A TRICK OF THE LIGHT

A TRICK OF THE LIGHT

Stories to Read at Dusk

JACKIE VIVELO

G. P. Putnam's Sons · New York

Library of Congress Cataloging-in-Publication Data
Vivelo, Jackie.   A trick of the light.
Contents: Reading to Matthew—The girl who painted
raindrops—A dog named Ransom—Night vision—[etc.]
1. Ghost stories, American. [1. Ghosts—Fiction.
2. Supernatural—Fiction. 3. Short stories] I. Title.
PZ7.V828Tr 1987 [Fic] 87-2492 ISBN 0-399-21468-2

CONTENTS

A TRICK OF THE LIGHT

READING
TO MATTHEW

I WAS FOURTEEN when my brother Matthew was knocked out one day at school. It was an accident that could have happened to anybody. But Matthew didn't regain consciousness. When they finally let me see him, he looked strange just lying there. I'd have tried anything I could think of to help, but a week passed before I thought of anything.

I couldn't seem to concentrate that week, not on school, not on television, not on books—especially not on books.

Matthew and I had been reading *The Call of the Wild* together; but, after I saw him and knew he couldn't listen any more, I lost interest. I couldn't bring myself to read it alone. You see, I've been reading to Matthew almost all his life.

My mom has a theory that you should start reading to kids as soon as they're born. She says she started reading to me before I left the hospital. I know for a fact that she was reading to the twins before they were a week old. When people try to tell her how dumb it is, she just waves her hand and says, "Look at my kids! They were all reading by the time they were four."

She also believes that kids can understand anything that someone takes the time to explain; "anything" includes cubism and the theory of relativity, as well as what's happening to water when it boils. I don't know how well her theories work, but they didn't seem to hurt me or the twins. The twins are my sisters Anne and Kate. When I was seven and they were five, Matthew was born.

Of course, Mom started him off just the way she did the rest of us. Then, when he was not quite two years old, she told us she was going back to work. She was glad about everything except Matthew. She said he would be well taken care of, but there wouldn't be as much time for her to read to him. And then she did it.

"John," she said to me, "I'm going to make it your responsibility to read to Matthew every day. Read him everything you can for as much time as you can."

That was fine with me. For one thing I liked Matthew, at least better than I liked Kate and Anne. Also, since I was oldest, it seemed like a good thing for me to have more responsibility.

The twins are supposed to have done everything faster than I did, walking, talking, tying their shoelaces. Now here was Matthew breaking their records. I liked that. At eighteen months, he already had a pretty big vocabulary and sometimes spoke in sentences. I thought if I could teach him to read by the time he was three, ol' Kate and Anne would die of shame.

I remember the very first thing I read to Matthew. It

44

was Beatrix Potter's *The Tale of Tom Kitten*. Now, Mom had been reading him *Time* magazine and an Agatha Christie novel. When he was really small, she would put him in this little cloth carrier thing and let him ride around with her while she worked. She read to him from a recipe book, circulars that came in the mail, letters from my grandparents, anything.

Well, just about the time she asked me to start reading to him, he had been given a set of those really little books Beatrix Potter wrote, and I figured it would be nice for him to hear a story that made some sense for a change. So I took two or three of them, and Matthew and I went outside to read. I showed him a picture at the start of the Tom Kitten book and began to read. He looked at every picture just as soon as I turned the page, but I couldn't tell if he was enjoying the story. He didn't make a sound.

Well, I finished reading the story, and Matthew slapped his fat little hands onto his fat little knees and said, "Again."

I turned back to the front of the book and read the whole story over again. When I finished, Matthew slapped his knees and nodded his head and said, "Read again."

When the same thing happened over again, I thought maybe this was like the throwing-the-spoon-out-of-the-high-chair trick. You know, when the kid drops his spoon so you can hand it back. Then he drops it again so you will hand it back again. Two things babies love are repetition and getting you to do things for them. I reminded myself that no matter how smart he was, Matthew was still a baby. Anyway, I showed him the other books, which looked like the one we had been reading, and suggested we try *The Tale of Peter Rabbit*.

He said, "Okay," with a big nod and sat there holding his hands on his knees like a little old man.

He leaned forward to study the pictures; just like before he didn't make a sound or move an inch when I started to read. This time though I began to get a funny feeling. When I came to the part about going "lippity— lippity—not very fast," I knew I was reading but I felt it too. I mean I could feel big, strong hindlegs pushing me along in sort of gentle loppety motion. I turned the page. (I could still turn the page and I was still reading the words.) The drawing on the next page was all around us. I know I'm not explaining this right, but how would you explain it? I mean I was reading the book but I knew I was *in* the book too. I looked at Matthew and just then he wiggled his fat little rabbit body under a wooden fence and I had to crawl under after him and keep reading at the same time. This time he didn't have to ask; we read the book over three—maybe four—times.

When we finally stopped and went back into the house, I didn't believe what had happened. It didn't make sense, so I just didn't believe it. And, of course, Matthew didn't tell anybody. For one thing he didn't think anything strange had happened, although he did tell me I read better stories than Mom. For another thing, even if he had known that stories weren't sup- posed to come alive like that, he couldn't have explained what had happened. He had a good vocabulary but not that good.

For part of every day I took Matthew outside to read to him. After a while I stopped not believing and began to understand that reading to Matthew was not like any other reading I had ever done. I thought maybe there was something really strange about that set of Beatrix Potter books.

We read the whole set. I knew just what it felt like to be in a hole underground with Mrs. Tittlemouse, how Mr. Jackson's toothless toad mouth looked, how beeswax smelled, and what honeydew tasted like. I got to know all the sights, sounds, smells, and tastes of Thomasina Tittlemouse's house because she was one of Matthew's favorites. We only read *The Story of a Fierce Bad Rabbit* once. Being shot at was too scary.

Sometimes, Mrs. Holt, the lady who stayed with us during the day, would be in our kitchen ironing. And Matthew and I would go outside and read about Mrs. Tiggy-Winkle, who would also be ironing. The smell of the hot iron on the damp clothes was just the same— inside the house and inside the story.

I don't know how my mother finally came to notice that I wasn't reading anything but Beatrix Potter, but toward the end of the summer she told me I'd either have to start reading other things or she'd put the twins in charge of Matthew's reading. She said if I just stuck with "those tiny books" because I resented reading to the baby I should say so.

I told her I was reading those books because they were

what Matthew liked, and Matthew jumped in and said, "They's Matthew's best stories."

"You see, you're stunting his vocabulary. He isn't talking any better than he was two months ago."

"Don't you be silly, you silly old mom," Matthew told her in Mrs. McGregor's words from a book about the flopsy bunnies.

"He doesn't mean to be calling you silly," I said quickly. "He's just showing you some words he has learned."

"I don't think I like the words he has been learning." She was studying his face. She pulled her eyes away, and said firmly to me, "Start on *Winnie-the-Pooh* tomorrow."

"Sure," I agreed. "I'll get out the Pooh books tonight."

We must have spent two or three weeks reading *Winnie-the-Pooh*. At first it was just like reading had always been—before I began reading to Matthew. Then one day, after we'd finished reading, Matthew asked me which stick I thought really won in the Poohsticks game.

"Well, Piglet's was the crooked one."

And then it hit me. I was seeing the game, picturing it the way I had watched it happen. I focused on the stream in my memory and counted the sticks as they appeared out of the shadow of the bridge. There were two extra sticks: Matthew and I had been in the game. The Pooh stories were different from the Beatrix Potter ones. We never got into the Five Hundred Acre Wood while we were reading, but after we put the book aside we could "remember" things as though they'd happened to us.

Over the next year we read some books that came to life and some that didn't. You really get into some stories but some are just there to be read.

During the school year, I didn't read to Matthew so often. By the time he was four, Matthew could read simple books for himself.

Sometimes he'd bring me a picture book and say, "Read, John."

"Matthew," I'd say, "it's mostly just pictures. You read it."

The book would hang at his side and he'd shake his head.

"It not the same, John. It doesn't read for Matthew."

When Matthew was five or six, I got interested in pirates and was reading *Treasure Island*. He kept pestering me to read, so to keep him quiet I started reading my book out loud to him. I didn't go back to the beginning and start over for him. I just picked up right where I was and read from there.

I had been letting this kid *beg* me to read to him? I soon realized I ought to be paying him to listen to me read. *Treasure Island* had been a good book before; suddenly it was great.

I hadn't read a full page out loud before I found myself inside an apple barrel. Sure, I could see the page in front of me and I was still reading, but I could also see the rough staves of the apple barrel. I could hear Jim

Hawkins breathing beside me, and I could feel Matthew's hand on my arm. All around us was a smell like apple cider. Just beyond us, on the other side of the barrel, was Long John Silver, his voice deep and honeyed-sounding.

Once in a while when we were going to read, Kate and Anne would sit beside us saying "Read to us, too."

"No," Matthew would say, "you go away."

"We want to listen too," Anne would wail.

"No, John reads to Matthew," Matthew would tell them.

While we couldn't get "into" some books no matter how hard we tried, in others a whole world would open up. The place, the characters, everything that happened would be real.

And all the time we were reading, Matthew was growing up. I was never sure how much he understood of the novels I liked to read now, but when you're living the story what difference do a few five-syllable words make?

By the time Matthew was seven and I was fourteen, we were both reading different sorts of books on our own. And still, books only became real for me when I was reading out loud to Matthew. I suspected that was also the only time the magic worked for him too. So, of course, I found time to read to him.

From the very start, *The Call of the Wild* was a funny book. What I mean is that it drew us into it in strange ways. Sometimes I could feel the warmth of a parka around me and could feel myself sliding over the packed, frozen snow at the back of a sled. At other times as I read I could feel my feet striking the crusted snow and the straps of a harness biting into my shoulders as I raced along as part of the team pulling the sled. I never knew who I'd be or where I'd be in the story.

We'd gotten about two-thirds of the way through the book when Matthew was hit by a ball and ended up unconscious in the hospital.

At first, Anne and Kate and I weren't allowed to see him. Even when they told us he wasn't going to die, only the adults could go in.

"He's okay though, isn't he, Mom?" Kate asked.

Mom just started to cry. Finally, my dad said, "He doesn't know us. He's fine, except that he doesn't know us. He doesn't know anything."

"Amnesia?" Anne said wonderingly.

"Unconscious" isn't amnesia, but I knew how she felt. I mean stuff like that doesn't *really* happen.

"The doctors say it may take time," Dad said.

"Or it may take forever," my mom added angrily. "It's as though it's Matthew but not Matthew." She was crying again.

Later that day, we three kids got to see Matthew, but only just see him. We weren't allowed to stay at all.

A week later he was still in the hospital and nothing had changed. The doctors said that there was no reason he shouldn't recover but that head injuries are strange things.

"I know he'll be all right," Mom said that evening. "It's just as though his mind were wandering off in some other realm."

I fell asleep that night thinking of what she'd said, imagining Matthew's body here and his mind somewhere else. All that night I had crazy dreams. Time after time I could see Matthew just ahead of me. I'd almost reach him and then he'd slip away. In one dream we were rabbits, and then we were boys tumbling past the roots of a tree into the ground. In a later dream that same night I chased Matthew through foggy London streets. Then, dodging pirates on a sandy beach, I looked for Matthew on an island.

I woke up the next morning determined to get Matthew back. If he was lost somewhere outside himself, I meant to find him.

"I want to visit Matthew," I said at breakfast. "I want to go and read to him."

Everybody objected. They argued that you can't read to somebody who's unconscious.

I didn't argue. I just kept saying, "I want to go read to Matthew."

And finally they agreed. I didn't care that it was a schoolday, but my parents did. They said I could go to the hospital as soon as school was over. I had to accept that, but I didn't think about anything else all day.

When school was over, my dad picked me up and drove me to the hospital. I asked him to leave me there.

"I'll be back around six," he told me.

Beside Matthew's bed, I took a long look at my brother. He was a round-faced little kid, but not pudgy like he'd been as a baby. I watched the short fingers of his hand lying on the sheet. I was really seeing him. He had always just been my "brother," the baby-faced kid I read to.

A clear picture came to me of an afternoon we'd spent—me and Matthew, Alan Breck and David Balfour—in the hollowed-out top of a tall rock. There'd been soldiers swarming all around on the ground below our rock searching for us. It was as much as our lives were worth for anyone to realize that we were there, the four of us, right above them.

Matthew had gripped my arm and said, "He'll get us out safe, won't he? Alan Breck would never let the soldiers catch us."

He'd called him "Ah-lan," broadening the "a" and rolling the name just the way Alan himself would say it and his eyes had shone with hero worship. I hadn't felt jealous then, but I guess I did standing beside the hospital bed. I needed to be as big a hero as Alan Breck in *Kidnapped*, bigger really, because Alan Breck was a showoff. He'd get you into trouble and then pull you out so you'd be grateful and admire him for it. Still, I wished he was here now.

I pulled a chair right up to the head of the bed and opened the copy of *The Call of the Wild* that I'd brought with me.

Just the day before he'd been hit by that ball Matthew had been with me in the frozen northland. I didn't know where he might be now, but this was the only way I knew how to search for him.

I began to read, "Late next morning Buck led the long team up the street. There was nothing lively about it, no snap or go in him and his fellows. They were starting dead weary."

I read three full pages and all that happened was that

I was mouthing words from the printed page. Nothing I'd ever read alone had come to life for me. I needed Matthew and he wasn't there.

My mother had cried for the first few days after Matthew was hit. Kate and Anne had cried loudly and wetly that first night. I hadn't cried. But now sitting there reading out loud to a kid who couldn't hear me, I felt my eyes get wet. I wouldn't let a tear fall. I just kept reading. Pretty soon my nose started running, and I had to keep wiping it on my hand.

Then I started reading and talking to Matthew at the same time. I was saying, "I know you're here, Matthew. Come on, let me see you." Then I would read another line or two just to keep the story moving. Then I'd say, "I need to find you, Matthew. We've got to stay together. We're in this together. I'm here with you." And then I'd read some more.

I don't know when I began to feel the drop in the temperature, but that was the first change. I was cold. I kept talking and I kept reading.

The wind seemed to be hitting my face at gale force so I had trouble keeping my eyes open. Still I kept reading. Snow seemed to be sticking in my hair—no, my fur, the fur that covered me. I gulped a deep, relieved breath of icy air. I was in the story. I read of the dogs racing over the ice, and I felt my feet, my *four* feet, striking the hard, cold surface.

Just in front of me I could see the big, powerful haunches of a Saint Bernard, and I knew I was right behind Buck, who was leading the team.

"Matthew!" I inserted the cry into the printed text

and tried to look around me. I didn't have far to look. My teammate, the sled dog harnessed in beside me, was short with powerful legs and such a fluffy, fuzzy coat that it looked like puppy fur. I recognized my brother in a single glance.

I choked on a laugh and kept reading and running.

After a few pages of icy racing, the team was pulled to a halt and unhitched. Night was falling fast when someone threw us meat. I dug a hole below the snow and Matthew and I curled up in shared warmth. Night lasted less than the space of a paragraph, but it was a night just the same.

How am I going to get us out of here? I wondered. Always before just to stop reading had been enough, but to stop reading now might take me out of the story leaving Matthew behind. I had found him, and I wasn't going to lose him again.

What if I was doing the wrong thing? Maybe I was pushing Matthew beyond his own physical limits. The animals were so underfed and overworked that the entire team was near exhaustion. And things were growing steadily worse.

Just about then, John Thornton appeared in the story—a hero, at least a hero for Buck.

"If you strike that dog again, I'll kill you," I said, speaking John Thornton's words.

As always I could see the printed page in front of me even as I felt ice forming on my fur. I forced myself to look ahead in the story.

Halfway down the page my eyes caught the words that spelled disaster. Within the next few lines John Thornton would separate Buck from his cruel master, and a line or two after that the whole team, all the dogs except Buck, would go hurtling to their deaths when the icy bottom of the trail dropped out.

I had already been mixing my own words with those of the story. I decided to try it again.

"I'm John Thornton," I said out loud, adding the assertion to the story. "My name is John Thornton," I repeated.

I could see Buck stretched out on the snow where the man called Hal had been thrashing him, and my view of him seemed changed from the moment before. The team was changed too. The dogs were harnessed in single file. Behind Buck there was now only one sled dog, the fuzzy, half-grown pup I'd recognized as Matthew. Where was I?

Struggling to get my bearings, I read on. Hal drew his long hunting knife. And, as I saw it, I knew he meant to kill the man who stood between him and the dog he had been beating. He meant to kill John. His hatred was so strong I could feel it, almost even see it like hot breath in cold air. As it touched me, I knew it was hatred toward me.

I am John, I thought. *Of course, it's me he wants to kill.*

I brought my hand down hard across his knuckles, knocking the knife to the ground. Then I added something else to the story, saying the words out loud, acting and describing the action at the same time.

"John picked up the knife and with two strokes cut Buck's traces, and then with two more swift strokes severed the traces of the fuzzy, young sled dog behind Buck. . . . Hal had no fight left in him." I picked up the story and continued it just the way Jack London wrote it. Only this time a stocky young sled dog had joined John and Buck to watch in safety as the people and the team disappeared through the ice a quarter of a mile down the trail.

And this time when John Thornton reached out saying "You poor devil," he reached with both hands and met the fur of *two* half-frozen dogs.

I felt the thick fur of the young dog's neck beneath my fingers. Relief made me weak. The sled dog that was Matthew was safe, but again I wondered if I had been a fool to try to reach my brother this way. I had found him, even touched him, somewhere out there in the no-man's-land of Jack London's Alaska. I hoped it hadn't done any harm.

The reunion between Buck and John Thornton was followed right away by the destruction of the sled and that ended the chapter. I knew I'd have to go on, but just for the moment I stopped, wondering what other traps might lie ahead of us.

Slowly I closed the book, holding my place with my finger, and then I closed my eyes. I had to wipe my nose again.

"John?"

I opened my eyes and looked around in disbelief. Matthew had raised his head and was looking at me, clear-eyed and knowing.

"Aren't you going to read any more of it, John?"

THE GIRL WHO PAINTED RAINDROPS

"THERE'S A SORT of magic about some pictures. It's as though the picture knows a secret," said Rachel, adding touches of foam to a stormy sea.

"What do you mean?" her sister Clara asked.

"I don't know how to explain it. Sometimes I look at a picture and I think it's hiding something, something I can't see. But the whole picture sort of hints at what's there."

Clara came to stand behind her sister and, turning her head to one side, studied the painting Rachel was working on.

"You mean something like the boat that's hidden behind that wave," she offered thoughtfully.

"Oh, you knew it was there too! I'm glad."

"Girls, come down," their mother's voice called out. "Aunt Cheryl and Lois are here."

Leaving her easel behind, Rachel raced downstairs with her sister.

At nineteen, Lois was four years older than Rachel and seven years older than Clara. Already, she was a student of the famous Professor Le Brun, who was probably the most respected art teacher in the world.

For a while the girls and their mother listened to Aunt Cheryl talk about her cruise to the Galapagos while they ate Mother's special, very flat, fried sandwiches and drank lemon tea.

Then Lois began to talk about her studies, how fabulous Monsieur Le Brun was and how impossible to please and what an honor it was to be allowed to study with him because he wouldn't accept more than one of every five hundred students who came to him.

Before Rachel could stop her, Clara blurted out, "Rachel is a painter, too. Her paintings are beautiful! I bet your professor would let *her* study with him."

Rachel wanted to hide. Although she liked her aunt and her cousin, she knew that bragging was their biggest joy in life. They wouldn't like to have anyone else intruding on their favorite boasts. And Lois's artistic talent was certainly a favorite boast.

"Oh? How nice." Aunt Cheryl gave her a beaming smile, then turned to her mother and asked, "Is there any more tea?"

And yet somehow before they left, both Aunt Cheryl and Lois were led upstairs to look at Rachel's paintings.

When she realized she couldn't avoid having her pictures looked at, Rachel chose only a few to share. She showed a painting of the mountains looking dark blue against a blue sky, and a picture of a clear gray window with silver raindrops running down the outside of the glass and a spiderweb on an inside corner, and finally her new painting of gray sea below gray clouds.

"They're magical paintings," loyal Clara said.

"Well, isn't Rachel the smart one!" Aunt Cheryl said. "How old are you now?"

Lois just looked and acknowledged that the pictures were "nice."

Rachel felt as though she had been patted on the head.

As soon as they were gone, Rachel said, "Mother, how could you insist that they look at my paintings?"

"It can't hurt for them to realize you have talent too. And perhaps Lois will mention you to her professor."

Rachel did not think that was at all likely. Even if the professor did hear of her, what good would it do? One of the things Aunt Cheryl had included in her list of brags was how many thousands of dollars they were paying Professor Le Brun to give lessons to Lois. As much as she loved art and would like to study with someone like the professor, Rachel knew her family couldn't afford his fees, even if he would accept her as a student, which of course he wouldn't anyway.

Several months later a phone call came from Lois. Her professor had an opening for another student, and Lois had described Rachel's work to him. The professor wanted to see Rachel and a sample of her work. Rachel would have to understand that there would be thousands trying for the same opening. Would she come?

"Yes, of course," Mother said and hung up before Rachel could raise any of the ten objections that sprang to mind.

"I haven't finished school," Rachel said, picking one problem out of many.

"You can finish school there. He hasn't accepted you anyway," Mother argued. "We will worry about when, where, how—*if* and only if he accepts you as a student. You have talent, but you may never really be an artist if you stay here. This is a chance. You must take it."

So Rachel painted a new picture especially for the professor and packed her things for a two-day visit. The following week she boarded the train at their little mountain junction and began her trip to the city.

She almost took a seat beside a man smoking a strong cigar, but she noticed the smell just in time to turn aside and sit down beside a small, white-haired man who was dozing, undisturbed by the train's brief stop at Rachel's depot.

Rachel was sorry that the little man had the window seat, but she contented herself with looking past him into the mist of the early morning fields to watch trees speed past and the mountains beyond slowly roll along. After a while she turned her attention into the rail car and looked over her fellow travelers. A little girl tugging at her mother's sleeve saw Rachel looking her way, immediately dropped the sleeve, and squirmed down from her seat to come and stand beside Rachel.

"What's your name? Mine's Susan."

"I'm Rachel. Where are you going, Susan?"

"To see my grandmother in the city."

In a few moments, Rachel had learned that Susan was four, her little brother was two, and they lived on a farm some twenty miles beyond Rachel's town.

Rachel, in turn, had to explain that she was going to the city to find out if she could study art there.

"What do you paint?" Susan asked, having managed to seat herself on Rachel's lap.

"I paint clouds and spider webs and mist. See the mist above those trees? It has been steadily rising all the time we've been rushing along. Wouldn't you like to catch it and keep it?"

Susan made a face at Rachel.

"You can't catch mist."

"No, but I can paint it. I can put it in a picture and keep it."

"What else do you paint?"

"I like raindrops and storm clouds and waves. I like to paint things that don't last, like colors in the sky."

"Is that a picture?" Susan pointed to the wrapped package in front of Rachel.

"Yes," Rachel answered reluctantly, knowing what was coming next.

"Please let me see."

As Rachel hesitated, trying to think of a way to refuse that would not send the child crying to her mother, another voice cut in.

"Yes, let us see the painting. A girl who paints raindrops shouldn't hide them."

Startled, Rachel turned to find the old man was now awake, though his head still rested against the back of the seat. His pale gray eyes were watching her, and Rachel wondered how long he had been listening.

"I'm sorry. I don't think . . ."

"Your package there is only tied. We have no seals to break. Slip the cord off and let us see this famous painting."

Rachel could have said no, but there was something very tempting in the eager interest of the old man and the little girl. Because she was a little frightened thinking of the judgment to come, she liked the idea of sharing her picture with uncritical admirers. So, setting Susan back on the floor of the car, she reached for her picture. Sliding the cords aside, she unwrapped the brown paper and held up the painting.

At first glance it looked like an abstract painting, all soft grays with a streak of golden-orange.

"What is it?" Susan asked.

"Look at it and tell me what you think it is."

"I think . . ." Susan hooked an index finger over her lower teeth. "It's the sky in the early morning, and that's our mountains."

Rachel smiled, looking into the painting past layers of mist to the mountains and above the dark mountains to the gray sky with clouds barely visible and the horizon touched by the first hint of sun.

"Let me," said the old man, lifting it from Rachel's hands and turning the canvas toward the window.

He tilted it once or twice, looked at it head-on and from angles. Then with a gruff grunt, he handed it back to Rachel.

Rachel tried to believe he was still grumpy from sleep. Besides, what would somebody's old grandfather—or a little girl for that matter—know about art? Shrugging off her disappointment, she bundled her mist-shrouded dawn back into its wrapper. Susan helped her tug the cord into place, patted her arm, and said, "Pretty picture."

When Susan returned to her own seat, Rachel closed her eyes intending just to rest. Soon, however, she fell asleep. She had hardly slept at all for the past two nights because she had been so excited over her trip.

Of course, she couldn't really begin to study art, not so far from home or with such an expensive teacher. But the excitement lay in showing a painting to someone who actually knew about art, someone who could tell her if her paintings were as good as she believed they were. It was exciting and scary too.

"You like to capture the things that will not last. You dipped your paint brush in the morning mist and captured water in the oil of your canvas."

Rachel was blushing with the warmth of the professor's praises when a sudden jolt of the train woke her up.

The old man who had been sitting beside her was gone. Susan's mother was handing out sandwiches and hard-boiled eggs from a basket. Clearly, it was lunchtime. Rachel got out her own lunch packet and began to eat.

Time passed and the old man did not return from the dining car or wherever he had gone. Susan visited again, crawled into the vacant seat and fell asleep.

At last the train rolled into Rachel's stop. She returned Susan to her mother and gathered up her things.

Lois, together with three friends, was waiting to meet her on the platform.

"This is the little genius," Lois said, introducing her. "Talent straight from the hills. Unschooled, of course, but brilliant."

Rachel couldn't imagine any good response to such an introduction, but her silence didn't matter because as they all five crowded into the car, Lois and her classmates began to talk to each other about their own interests, ignoring Rachel. She knew that to them she must seem like an ignorant, tongue-tied child from the mountains.

For a bit she tried to follow the bright chatter of the girls in the car. She noted the chrome yellow of a shirt, the red and indigo sweater, a chartreuse blouse shot through with fuchsia. The girls were as bright and electric as their clothes. Then Rachel found she was losing track of the conversation as she tried to see the buildings they were passing. When she tried to recapture the thread of the discussion, she realized there wasn't one but two or even three conversations, almost one per person. But none of them included her.

She had wondered how her self-centered cousin had ever come to recommend her to Professor Le Brun. Now quietly squashed in a corner of the back seat, she thought she understood. She was her cousin's "discovery," something else to brag about but of no importance in herself.

Rachel was sorry she had come. Lois and her friends might see themselves as arty and superior but in Rachel's eyes they were loud and rude and their professor—their rich, fashionable professor—would surely be like them. What could he know—shut in the geometrical city, surrounded by bright, painted people—of the quiet things Rachel liked to paint?

When looking and listening became more than she

could manage, she pictured to herself a green painting she had done: green, moss-covered rocks; green leaves and vines; a close-up view of a little bit of hillside. Water was trickling over the rocks and over the leaves and vines in the picture, water that had itself turned green from all the greenness it had washed over. A single drop had formed at the tip of one leaf and was just about to fall.

"Here we are!" Lois called out. "Grab your things, Rachel, and bring them up to my room."

Lois, it turned out, had a small apartment to herself, but her friends all lived in rooms in the same building. In Lois's sitting room, Rachel spent another hour hovering at the edge of things until the three visitors finally scattered to their rooms.

Left to themselves, Lois and Rachel had little to say. As a guest, Rachel could think of nothing she felt free to do. Lois, however, feeling no similar uneasiness at trespassing, unsnapped the locks on Rachel's suitcase.

"Here, let's see what you've brought." Deftly, she sifted through the clothes. Her handling of them and her expression conveyed her disdain. "I think we'll shake this one out. Maybe it will be okay for this evening."

"Will I see Professor Le Brun this evening?"

"No, we're not seeing him until tomorrow, but some of us are going out for a party tonight. Is that the painting you brought? Let's have a look at it."

And just as she had done with the suitcase, Lois made short work of opening up the painting. A little shiver ran through Rachel, but this—she told herself—was what it would be like if she wanted to paint for other people. Besides, Lois, wise from her sophisticated study, would appreciate the subtle painting Rachel had brought.

The paper came away from the painting, and Lois exclaimed, "Oh, no! What is this?"

Rachel was stunned. Lois was not only talented, she was trained. She belonged right in the heart of an art school that Rachel had only dreamed about. She must know what she was talking about.

"Why didn't you bring that window with the cobweb? I wanted to show Professor Le Brun that I can spot talent—even if it's crude and untrained. If he sees this, he'll think I have no judgment at all."

Lois clicked her tongue and shook her head in dismay, clearly anticipating embarrassment and shame in front of her friends.

Why hadn't she brought something everyone would recognize? Why had she tried to be clever?

"Well, it won't do," Lois continued, sparing one pitying glance for Rachel. "But maybe we can still save it. Some sort of sun-on-the-horizon thing, isn't that what it's supposed to be?"

She put aside the wrapping paper and set the painting on an easel. In a sort of frozen horror, Rachel watched as Lois got out her paints and brushes and stood in thought in front of the canvas.

"But it was meant to . . ." Rachel's voice came out so choked with emotion that she couldn't be sure Lois had heard her.

"I suppose it's a sunrise," Lois was saying. "It could be almost anything."

"No!" Rachel cried, as Lois swirled a brush in bright color, horror giving way to anger at her cousin's presumption.

"It'll be okay," Lois said over her shoulder. "Some color will help."

With strong, sweeping brush strokes, she added crimson, gold, and streaks of yellowy-orange.

"Now *there's* a sunrise. And you see," she added considerately, "I've kept the outline of your mountains and those are your clouds. Your composition was good, but you need to learn to use color."

Rachel felt as sullied and ruined as her painting. By a reflex of politeness, she excused herself from her cousin's evening plans, pleading tiredness. As soon as she was alone she wrapped herself in her disappointment and went to bed. Thinking over the day, she was angry with herself for ever having made such a stupid and now pointless trip.

Suppose the professor loved the painting? It was no longer hers. He wouldn't be seeing her work at all. Nothing he said would matter. Even if he wanted her as a pupil, it would be under false pretenses. She wouldn't accept.

She briefly considered getting up, using a small canvas of Lois's and starting a new painting. But this place felt all wrong to her. What difference did it make, she asked herself miserably. And, thinking she would be awake all night, she rolled over and slept.

The next morning she was up, showered, and dressed before Lois woke. Rachel thought about trying to catch an earlier train and just leaving, but she knew she could not afford carfare to the station and Lois would never agree to drive her before she had seen Professor Le Brun. However awful it would be, she had to go through with meeting the professor.

As the time for her appointment with the professor drew near, Lois's three friends from the day before began to arrive.

"They're coming along for moral support," Lois explained.

One by one the girls examined and commented on the still-wet oil painting. No one mentioned Lois's contribution, but Rachel could tell by her cousin's smirk and the rolling of her eyes at the praise that she had told them all about how she had "saved" Rachel's miserable flop.

One of the girls, bending close, observed, "You know, the mountains almost look like they're bathed in mist," and a spark of feeling flickered in Rachel.

At last they were all ready. Her painting in her hand and her heart in her shoes, Rachel walked with them down the block to the gray stone building where Professor Le Brun held his classes. They went into an open, sunlit studio, a huge room with long tables and big open spaces, to wait for the professor.

Rachel knew she would have been excited if the painting now resting on an easel in a pool of sunlight had still been her own. Now she only felt numb, as though her senses had been muffled. She had been more interested in the little girl Susan's reaction yesterday than in the professor's today.

The glass-topped door of the room was thrown back with a violence that only just spared the glass. Rachel jumped at the sound and almost against her will glanced at the newcomer.

He was dressed in a black cape that swirled about him. A black hat and white gloves completed his costume. "Costume" was the word in Rachel's mind. She had no doubt that this was the great professor.

He paused dramatically and looked from girl to girl until he stopped at Rachel. She couldn't judge his expression because his face was shadowed by the brim of his hat.

After a long pause, during which Lois and her friends were silent, he turned to the easel.

Rachel leaned against one of the long tables and looked at her feet.

"Hmm," the professor said. Then after a long wait, "Ummm."

Rachel looked up. He had picked up the canvas and was studying it as though he thought he would find it full of bugs.

He isn't going to like it, she thought, and she was pleased.

The waiting seemed to go on forever. Then just when she thought she would have to sit down no matter what, the professor turned back to the girls.

"Who did this?" he asked.

"This is Rachel Parker," Lois said, making the name sound apologetic. "She's the one I told you about, my little cousin from—"

"No!" the professor thundered. "I am asking who sprayed mustard and catsup all over these mountains."

"Ah . . . why . . . uh . . ."

"Do not tell me. I know. Now go. Get out of here."

Hastily the girls fled toward the door.

"Not you," the professor said, stopping the group in midflight. "You there, the little one, come back here."

Rachel let the others slip through the door without her. Then, slowly, she moved toward the professor.

When she stopped before him, he said, "How did you let this monstrosity happen?"

"I'm sorry for wasting your time," she stammered. "I know I don't belong here."

"Now *that* I agree with. But this—this," he waved a hand at the sunrise-sunset. "This is not the picture as *you* painted it, is it, heh?"

"No, I didn't mean to be dishonest. Lois—Lois meant to help."

"And do you think she 'helped' your picture?"

"No, I hate it!" Rachel said, all her anger spilling into the words.

"You think your picture was better?"

"At least it was *my* picture. No, I don't want to be modest. Of course, it was better. It was beautiful."

"And even if *I* told you that it was very bad, would you still think it was beautiful?"

"Even if you thought it was bad, I would still know it was beautiful," Rachel said, pushed by her anger into more courage than she had ever had before. "But how could you ever know if it was good or bad? It's ruined now."

"Perhaps. But I can see through paint. It speaks to me. And this picture is crying out in pain. Look here." A swift finger jabbed. "And here. Those are the brush strokes of one painter. These are of another. The painting, the original and *dry* painting, is very fine work. And that work is yours, isn't it?"

"Yes."

"A very soft 'yes.' Where is the courage of a moment ago? 'Yes, Monsieur Le Brun, and be damned to your opinion.' I liked that. And I liked the mountains and the mist and the single ray of light. Just touching the clouds here, wasn't it?"

"You really can see through paint!"

The big man tipped back his head and laughed.

"Perhaps. Perhaps. But I knew when I saw this painting yesterday that you were a girl who puts magic in her paintings."

"But you . . ." She peered below the shadowing hat searching for a glimpse of the gray eyes or the white hair of the little man from the train. Little man? This man was much larger. "I don't think . . ."

"No, you don't remember me. It was only my cigar you noticed yesterday. It's always good for keeping a whole seat to myself."

When Rachel caught the train for home that evening, she was still filled with the sort of glow that comes from being appreciated. Professor Le Brun would take her as a pupil; in fact, he wouldn't take no for an answer. And she did not need to leave school or to come to the city.

Studying her picture together, looking beyond its catsup and mustard, she and the professor had talked about her mountains.

"There is a house right here," he had asserted. "Just behind this fold of the mountains."

"Yes! My house, the house where I live is just there."

The professor not only could see through paint but could read the secrets of paintings as well.

In return for two months of mountain air each year, he said to Rachel, he would come to her, to stay with her family in that little house in the mountains. Well, the plan would need her mother's approval of course, but she would agree, especially when Rachel explained that Monsieur Le Brun had promised never to smoke his cigars indoors.

A
DOG
NAMED RANSOM

T HE FIRST TIME Harry Norton ever saw Ransom, the dog was sitting up beside the driver on a mule-drawn wagon. Ransom sat up as high and was as black as the man; both of them rode straight with an easy, graceful sway.

Watching them, Harry decided that someday he'd own a mule and ride around with a big, proud-looking dog. He knew the man was coming to his house because his father had said he was hiring a man named Isaac to plow their back lot for them. Harry, who had never been shy, went out, introduced himself, and watched Isaac unhitch the mule.

"You gotta take him off the wagon every time you stop?"

Isaac gave a little shake before he answered. Or, maybe he was laughing.

"I got to unhitch him from the wagon so I can hitch him to the plow."

"He pulls your plow?" Harry, who was eight at the time, was amazed. He had expected somebody to come and plow with a tractor. Machines of any kind were the gods of his world. He'd been looking forward to the tractor.

"I don't hold with automation," was all Isaac answered.

Harry rolled the words around in his head a few times, and then tried them on his own tongue, but he couldn't match the ringing tone of Isaac.

When Isaac had unloaded the plow from the back of his wagon, Harry examined it, following with his hands the curving iron handles and the polished blades. He found on it the picture of a leaping stag.

"It has sharp blades."

"Almost as sharp as you. You run tell your dad I charge extra for nuisance."

"He's not here right now." Harry's father was an insurance agent who had an office downtown and also an office in his house. Most days he was downtown. "Anyway, what's 'nuisance'?"

Isaac shook in silence for a moment and then he grinned at Harry.

"One kind of nuisance is having to give on-the-job training to pint-sized whippersnees."

Harry thought that over for a while. "You mean me," he said at last. "Am I really bothering you?"

"Not to say 'bothering,' no. But you could be a hindrance when I start to plow."

"Maybe I could just sit here with your dog while you plow. What's his name? Do you think it'll take you long?"

"Depends on how hard and rocky that field is, all

morning I'd guess. No, you can't sit with my dog, but you can go introduce yourself. His name is Ransom and he'll shake hands if you ask him nice."

Harry walked up, told the dog his name and held out his hand. Ransom looked first at Isaac and then at a nod offered his paw.

"He shook my hand. Did you see that? Ransom shook my hand."

Isaac was now ready to plow.

"Look, Harry, you stay here on the shady side of the field. Each time I turn on this side, I'll answer one question, just one!"

Harry nodded his agreement and trotted off toward the trees.

"Giddap! Go on, Rosie. Giddap!"

As soon as Isaac was close enough to hear, Harry was ready with a question.

"How old is Ransom?"

"Be five in July."

"How old is the mule?"

"Rosie's eighteen. Old enough to vote."

"Don't you ever want a car?"

"Nope."

"What about trains? Everybody likes trains."

"I like 'em well enough, but they won't take me home, and I can't plow with one."

For every question, a furrow was plowed.

"You got any children?"

"I got children, and I got grandchildren."

"What kind of dog is Ransom?"

"He's part shepherd and part Doberman pinscher."

"Why'd you name him 'Ransom'?"

"Why'd they name you 'Harry'?"

Harry had to wait until Isaac came back again to answer.

"I was named for my granddad."

"Ransom was named for a song."

When Isaac reached the shade the next time, Harry told him, "Someday I want to own a dog like Ransom."

"You 'own' him, he won't be like Ransom. Me and Ransom's just friends."

All morning Isaac plowed with Ransom walking right beside him. At every turn on the shaded side of the field, Harry asked a question.

By noon, his machine-gods weren't as secure in their heavens.

All that summer Isaac came in from time to time to help work the garden. It seemed to Harry that Isaac's life must be just about perfect.

"Whatcha doin' when you leave here?" he asked one morning in August.

"Going fishing. I got a hankering for catfish to eat with a mess of greens."

"Do Ransom and Rosie go fishin' with you?"

"Sure do. I don't go anywhere Ransom and Rosie can't go. They have to wait outside, but they go to church with me too."

Harry wanted to go fishing with them but he didn't ask. Some questions are easier to ask than others.

More than a year passed before Isaac invited him to go fishing. In early spring of the year Harry was ten,

Isaac told Harry to walk along behind him as he plowed and to pick up the worms that the plow uncovered. Harry put some dirt into a plastic pail and collected the worms that came crawling out of the fresh-turned earth.

Harry went fishing with Isaac two or three times that summer. Rosie would stand waiting in the shade, and Ransom would lie on the bank beside them. At the end of the day, Isaac would drive Harry home in the wagon.

"Clean those fish yourself. A good fisherman doesn't turn his catch over to anybody else."

In the fall and winter, Isaac delivered firewood in his wagon. And that's how it happened that he knocked at the back door one Saturday in December and asked Harry to come outside.

"You hear that?" he asked, when Harry joined him by the newly stacked wood.

From a distance came a raucous sound of honking.

"What is it?"

"You just stand and watch."

Eyes and ears straining, Harry stood beside Isaac and Ransom and, like them, watched the sky. He saw it first as just a black line in the sky. Then slowly it grew into a deep V-shape. And, finally, he could make out the individual birds that made up the flying formation. Long necks outstretched, heavy bodies moving high above him, the Canada geese were flying south and making a terrific racket about it.

"They give you plenty of warning so you can get out and see them. When that V passes straight over you and when you see them and hear them right above you the way we just did, that's good luck for a whole year."

Harry could feel the good luck. He and Ransom and Isaac were all going to have a good year.

"Superstition," Harry's dad said that night at supper. "Superstition is like a game. It can be fun, but you don't want to start believing it's real."

One day in the following summer, Isaac and Harry fished while Ransom slept in the shady bank of the lake. Rosie cropped the grass while she waited to take them home.

In his sleep, the dog made noises deep in his throat. Occasionally, his feet made running motions.

"Think he's dreaming of rabbits?" Harry asked.

"Yes and no. He's after something—could be a squirrel or a possum just as easy as a rabbit. And it isn't exactly a dream."

Harry had done some reading about dreams and about animal intelligence as well, but he had as much faith in Isaac's observations and beliefs as he had in scientific research.

"If it's not a dream—I mean a dream like people have—what is it?"

"Out in the woods somewhere right now there's a real animal getting chased by a wraith of a dog. That animal's scared half out of his wits 'cause that great big something chasing him is Ransom's dream wraith."

Harry didn't comment. Most of Isaac's pronouncements weren't open to discussion. And, anyway, "dream wraiths" made as much sense as some of the articles he'd read.

That fall Harry's dad hired Isaac to do some yard work: plant a tree, take out a row of shrubs, and clear the undergrowth from another section of hedge. Isaac was finishing up the work on a Saturday when the whole family was going away.

"Don't you worry," he told Mr. Norton. "I understand what you want."

When Harry's family came back around five in the afternoon, they saw that Isaac had started a small fire to burn the debris he'd cleared out of the hedge. On the top of the burning pile was the tree Harry's dad had left to be planted.

Mr. Norton, more baffled than upset, stopped the car in the driveway and hurried over, Harry trailing close behind. Ransom left Isaac's side to come running to meet Harry.

"Isaac, you're burning my tree. I wanted that planted just where we took out the kids' swing set."

"I know you did, Mr. Norton, but I couldn't do that. If you look around behind the garage, you'll see I planted a tree just where you wanted one. I went out to the woods and I dug you up a nice big pine. It'll do right well for you there, and it's bigger than this tree."

"That's nice, except that I didn't want a pine. I bought this tree, and it's the one I wanted you to plant."

Isaac was shaking his head. "I couldn't do that."

"Why? Why couldn't you do it?"

"If I'd planted that cedar tree, as soon as it grew tall enough to shade your grave, you'd die. I couldn't plant it, not knowing that."

Harry's dad argued a bit more but there was no budging the old man. He'd done what he had to do, and he'd do the same all over again if necessary.

"Superstition!" Harry's dad said in disgust. But the days passed and he left the pine where Isaac had planted it, and he didn't buy any more cedars.

Over the summers Isaac and Harry fished the creek, the lake, and the river. Little by little, Harry learned as much as the old man could teach him about fishing, and that meant that Harry became a very good fisherman. Isaac and Rosie and Ransom became part of the pattern of Harry's childhood. He thought they were a permanent part of his life, but he was wrong.

The four of them shared their last fishing trip the summer Harry was thirteen. At the time it just seemed like any other afternoon of river fishing. As usual, Rosie was in the shade. Ransom's great length was stretched out in the sun where he occasionally growled or stirred in his sleep.

"What do you think?" Harry asked. "A rabbit, a possum, or a squirrel?"

"It could be a skunk," Isaac said, laughing.

It was their last fishing trip because that was the summer somebody shot Isaac. He was killed right beside his wagon, and Rosie and Ransom were the only witnesses.

That year was a time in Harry's life when he was trying to act grown-up, and he listened to the details with all the detachment he could muster.

On a late Sunday evening, Isaac had driven his wagon into the alley behind the 600 block of Wilson

Street. Apparently he had been out later than he'd expected to be and had stopped at that particular place because there was an outdoor hydrant where he could get water for Rosie before making the long ride out to his house in the country. He had picked the wrong time to stop. Grove's Liquor Store on Wilson Street was being burglarized. Police speculated that Isaac must have seen the burglar, who had broken in through the rear of the store from the alley.

Because he handled the insurance for the liquor store, Harry's dad knew all the details of the break-in/murder. Neither the robbery nor the murder would have been discovered before Monday morning if it hadn't been for Ransom. His howls had caught the attention of a passing patrol car. Rosie was hitched to the wagon; Isaac lay nearby with Ransom standing guard over him.

"Dad, I'd like Ransom to come live with us," Harry suggested.

"I don't know, Harry. Isaac's son is coming in from Chalmer's Mill today. He may want to keep Ransom."

"If he doesn't, could we take him? Would you ask?"

"Well, why not? I wouldn't want to see Ransom go to the pound either."

Isaac's son sold Rosie and the wagon and was glad to accept the offer of a home for Ransom. And so it was that Ransom came to live with Harry and his family. Even though five years had passed since he first met Isaac, Harry still remembered their morning of questions and answers.

He had never forgotten that Ransom wasn't "owned" but was a friend. They had both been Isaac's friends, so Harry made up his mind that he'd be a friend to Ransom.

Ransom, by Harry's figuring, was now about ten years old, but the dog was still in his prime. Until Isaac's death he had maintained a dignified friskiness. Now he looked to Harry as though he had changed somehow. The big pointed ears still stood erect. His broad forehead gave a look of intelligence to his large head and his wide-set eyes. He rarely barked; but, when he did, the sound was a strong, bass rumble that shook the walls. He wasn't droopy or dejected-looking. Harry tried to analyze where the difference lay. Finally, he decided there was something too alert about the set of the ears, too watchful about the eyes. Ransom didn't seem grief-stricken. He seemed to be a dog who was waiting, watching and listening, for something.

Maybe he thinks Isaac will come back, Harry thought. But after his friend was shot the dog had stood guard. A dog as smart as Ransom must know that Isaac was gone for good. *So what is he waiting for?* Harry kept wondering.

Ransom settled in well to life with Harry's family. After a few days Harry even persuaded the dog to sleep on the floor beside his bed. He began to hope that he might replace Isaac in Ransom's affections. Dogs are adaptable creatures. Ransom adapted, but he remained watchful.

One evening after supper, Ransom and Harry were

keeping Mr. Norton company in his office at home while he waited for a client.

"I remember when I was just a kid and saw him for the first time. I thought he was part wolf. Isaac told me he's half German shepherd and half Doberman."

"He's a handsome creature," Mr. Norton acknowledged. "It's lucky that he's so gentle."

A knock sounded at the outside door to the office, and the hair along Ransom's back stood up straight.

"That should be Mr. Grove, the man whose liquor store was robbed," Harry's dad said, as he rose to open the door. "Come in, Gerald," he said to the man outside the door. "This is my son Harry, and his dog Ransom."

Like a tightly coiled spring, Ransom sprang to his feet; a growl rose menacingly.

"Easy, boy. It's okay, Ransom." Harry caught the dog and spoke soothingly.

"I'm sorry about that, Gerald. He's usually a quiet dog."

Gerald Grove shifted uneasily. "He looks like a brute, not the kind of dog I'd like."

"A mutual feeling, obviously," Mr. Norton said lightly. "You'd better take him away, Harry."

Harry called, but Ransom stood his ground. He continued to bristle and alternated between vicious growls and high, hurt-sounding whimpers.

"Come on, boy," Harry demanded, catching Ransom's collar.

At last Ransom gave ground; he turned his body while

still fixing Mr. Grove in the glare of his huge, dark eyes. In a final snarl he showed his teeth. The sight of those fangs sent Mr. Grove backing up toward the door he'd just entered.

Harry tugged Ransom through the door at the opposite side of the room. As he turned to close it behind him, he saw a white-faced, trembling Mr. Grove.

"That dog's not safe," he was saying.

"Did you hear that, Ransom?" Harry asked the dog. "He doesn't think much of you. Why'd you have to go and act like that?"

Ransom was uneasy for the rest of the evening. As Harry prepared to turn the dog out for his last run of the day, he hesitated, thinking how strange Ransom had been. As a precaution, he snapped a leash on the dog's collar and went out with him; but Ransom made an easy, loping circuit of the yard and came quickly back in.

As was now his custom, the dog settled down on the rug beside Harry's bed when the boy was ready to sleep.

Several hours later, Harry woke to the sounds of soft growls and muted whimpers, typical noises of a sleeping dog, only louder and harder to ignore. Harry rolled to the edge of his bed, reached down, and stroked the dog.

"Good boy, Ransom. You must be after a real bear this time," he muttered sleepily.

Ransom's lip trembled and drew back in a snarl. A yip merged into a chest-rattling rumble.

"Easy, boy."

After several minutes of following each growl with a reassuring pat, Harry slid off the bed and sat on the floor beside Ransom's head. He stroked the raised fur and kept repeating, "Easy. Steady. It's all right, Ransom."

And still the dog slept.

The red, glowing numerals on Harry's bedside clock said 3:45. Harry thought about waking the dog. Then vaguely he felt that it might not be a good idea. If touching him and speaking to him hadn't wakened him, maybe it would be too much of a jolt. *Like waking a sleepwalker*, Harry thought.

At four o'clock, he was still beside Ransom, speaking softly.

The dog was rigid with tension under Harry's stroking hands.

"You must be tangling with a grizzly," he said again.

Just watching the terrible struggle was tiring but Harry was troubled and fought off sleep. Time and again the dog seemed to coil for some decisive spring; each time Harry concentrated all his energy on reassuring words and a gentle touch. Time and again he was relieved to feel the tension ease in the dog until the next surge of energy came.

Although Harry had no idea what was going on, it seemed like a death struggle. He could almost believe that each time he soothed the dog, he was pulling him back from some precipice.

Soon after five, Harry's head began to bob. He'd jerk into wakefulness every time it dropped. Then he'd murmur something to the dog and stroke the big furry shoulders. Finally, exhausted, he stretched out on the floor beside Ransom and fell asleep with one arm across the dog.

The next morning Harry was stiff from his hours on the floor, but Ransom didn't seem any worse for his nightmares. In fact, he seemed filled with energy.

"Wrestling bears peps you up," Harry told him.

During breakfast, the phone began to ring. Harry's dad took the call and his end of the conversation was a series of startled monosyllables.

He left almost immediately without explaining the phone call; but, after Harry took Ransom out for a long run after breakfast, he came home to find a message that his dad wanted to see him at his office downtown. Harry refused his mother's offer to drive. His dad hadn't said it was urgent; in fact, he hadn't said what it was about at all. Leaving Ransom in the house, Harry rode his bicycle into town.

Harry said "Hi," to Mrs. Jacobs at the desk in the outer office, and she told him to go on through to see his father.

"Hi, son. Come in and take a seat," Mr. Norton called out.

He gave Harry a preoccupied smile that quickly faded.

"What's up, Dad?"

"Harry, Mr. Grove was banging on the sheriff's door around five o'clock this morning. When the sheriff opened up, Grove started babbling that he'd shot Isaac."

"Mr. Grove shot Isaac? But it was Mr. Grove's store that was being robbed!"

"According to what Grove blurted out at dawn this morning, there wasn't any real break-in. He said something about Isaac seeing him breaking his own back door after he had already emptied his office safe and taken dozens of cartons out of the store. At least, that was his first story."

"I don't understand. Why do you say his 'first' story? Did he shoot Isaac or didn't he?"

"He says now that he didn't, that his confession was part of a nightmare experience."

"I don't understand."

"I don't understand either, son. But I think the best thing is for me to tell you Grove's whole story. He says that after he left our house last night he went back to his store where he worked over the books until the early hours of the morning. He claims the robbery hit him really hard, and he's struggling to hold things together until the insurance money comes through. That's why he came to see me yesterday evening; he wants to hurry things along.

"Anyway, he says that as he stepped out of his building to go home he heard growls that sounded to him like a wild animal. He stood there pressed against the wall in terror until a 'huge beast' emerged from the shadows. He called it a great, black dog but said it was more like a demon than a dog. For the next two hours he was at the mercy of this creature. He thought he would be killed and his body, like Isaac's, would be found behind his store.

"The dog apparently fastened itself onto his leg and dragged him, sometimes tossing him but always growling, until he was out of his mind with fear. He expected to be killed at any moment, but each time the dog stopped short of mortal injury. The animal pulled him out of the alley and dragged him halfway through town before he loosened his hold.

"At that point, Grove ran for his life to the sheriff where he blurted out that first story about killing Isaac. Now, he says that pure terror made him crazy and he had nothing to do with the robbery and murder. And," Mr. Norton took a deep breath, "he's now demanding that the sheriff send someone out to shoot the dog. He claims he recognized it."

"You mean he thinks it was Ransom, don't you?" Harry said, suddenly realizing why his father had sent for him.

"Yes," his father agreed.

"Well, it wasn't. Ransom was beside my bed all night."

"Are you sure? He might have gotten out after you fell asleep, and it's a fact that he did take a real dislike to Mr. Grove."

"He woke me up in the middle of the night. He was growling, scrabbling around in his sleep so much I couldn't sleep. —Oh, Dad, that's it! Isaac told me dogs' 'wraiths' travel outside their bodies while they sleep. Ransom didn't chase Mr. Grove; his dream spirit did!"

"Nonsense!" Mr. Norton cried out, perhaps more harshly than he'd intended. He immediately added, "I know you valued your friendship with Isaac and so did I. But you can't believe the superstitious ramblings of an old man."

"At any rate, Ransom *didn't* leave my room all night. I finally lay down on the rug beside him. The two of us were there until breakfast time this morning."

"I think we'd better go tell that to the sheriff."

Harry and his dad went over together to talk to the sheriff. Harry was careful not to mention dream wraiths, and he found he had plenty of reason to be grateful for the nightmare that had cost him sleep but enabled him to swear that Ransom had been by his side all through the night.

"What will this mean to Mr. Grove?" Harry asked his father that evening. "Do you think he'll still blame Ransom?"

"I think Mr. Grove is going to have too many problems to worry about without time left over to persecute a dog."

"Do you think that he's guilty? Won't the police believe his confession no matter what he says now?"

"Oh, I don't know about that. He'll probably be able to clear himself, but the police will be looking more closely into his whereabouts at the time of that burglary. And his insurance pay-off will be delayed. Even apart from the losses in the break-in, he's in real financial difficulties. Yes, Mr. Grove has some rough times ahead of him."

"Suppose he did rob himself, Dad. Why would he do a thing like that?"

"Well, he needs money quickly. He could have thought the insurance money would solve his problem.

If he robbed himself, he didn't really lose anything, stock or money, and he stands to gain the insurance money."

"I don't care about that. I just wish they'd find out whether or not he killed Isaac."

The following morning word came that Mr. Grove had shot himself while cleaning a gun. He was killed instantly. The story of his experience with the dog-demon and his confession of murder had not been made public. So, as the news of his death spread, most people agreed that it was probably a tragic accident.

"I guess we'll never know the truth of it now," Mr. Norton said.

But it seemed to Harry that the truth was obvious. The proof of it was in the sudden change in Ransom. The dog lost his wary look. He seemed once again as carefree and as playful as his dignity allowed.

"He feels at home now."

"He finally adjusted to us."

"He just needed some time to settle in," the other members of the Norton family said.

He avenged Isaac, and he knows it's over, Harry thought.

But he kept the thought to himself.

NIGHT VISION

W HEN I WAS younger, I used to play a game I called "shape-changing." In my bedroom, there's a big chair with a curved back, and from my bed the back of that chair is silhouetted against the window. Ever since I was about four I could see its curve as the hump of a camel's back or the round lump of an elephant's head, or any of dozens of other things. By concentrating, I could make out a complete object or create a whole animal. A fold of the curtain would be the elephant's trunk. The sleeve of a sweater left hanging over the edge of my desk would be its tail, and so on.

The game worked a little like those drawings that can be seen two different ways. You know the kind I mean: Is it a vase or the profiles of two people facing each other? Is it a hag or a beautiful woman?

Well, in the near-dark of my bedroom, I had a habit of shifting lines around, changing my perspective, and letting my eyes trick my brain. Or, was it my brain that tricked my eyes? It was my private, secret trick and I played it for ten years or so, entertaining myself when

I was sent to bed too early to fall asleep or when I couldn't fall asleep in strange surroundings.

But I played my game of fooling myself one time too many.

Returning from a visit with my grandparents last summer, we stopped off for one night to visit relatives I hadn't seen since I was a toddler and didn't remember. The house they lived in was my father's grandfather's house. And the people we were visiting were Dad's aunts and my great-aunts. As we rode along, Dad was telling Mom and me and my sister Karen things he remembered about visiting there while his grandfather was still alive. He said he and his brother used to climb onto the garden shed and use its roof as a tree house where they played Tarzan. He remembered a goldfish pond, a playhouse, and a rope swing.

"I don't suppose any of those things are left from my grandfather's day, but we loved to go there as kids."

"Will we get to play outdoors?" my sister asked.

It wasn't as silly a question as it may sound. She was only seven, and we had just come from our own grandfather's home, which is a brand-new apartment in a high-rise building in the city. We had hardly set foot outside the door the whole time we were there.

"The playhouse and the swing are probably gone by now, but it's a big yard with plenty of trees. You'll be able to play outdoors. And Aunt Lydia wrote that there's a riding stable across the road from them now. So, you can go horseback riding, Meredith," Dad added to me.

When we arrived at our destination, it was supper-time and Aunt Phyllis and Aunt Lydia hustled us in to eat before we had much chance to look around, but after we had eaten, I took Karen for a walk. The big yard was almost a wilderness of trees and shrubs, and Karen loved it. She kept racing off after fireflies and even brought two, one in each fist, back into the house with her. She let them go in the kitchen.

The aunts laughed. "Your dad used to do the same thing when he was a youngster, only he and his brother would turn them loose in their bedroom and lie awake watching them."

Karen begged to go back outside for more so that she could take them up to bed with her, but Mom vetoed that. There wasn't any question of sitting up late with the adults as I had done at my grandparents' house because the great-aunts made it plain that they considered nine o'clock a decent bedtime for everybody.

When Karen and I were shown to a second-floor bedroom at the back corner of the house, she claimed the bed beside the door, and I took the one by the window.

Unable to fall asleep right away, I turned to look out the window and was glad Karen had left this bed for me.

There was enough moonlight for me to see the stretch of lawn at this corner of the house. Fireflies, seen from my window, looked like little clouds of twinkling light moving among the trees. To play my shape-changing game the light must be just right: bright enough to show shapes, dark enough to wash out colors. The light on the lawn was perfect.

I stretched, put my arm on the windowsill, and rested my head against my arm. And then, for the last time, I began to play my familiar game, rearranging the shapes of things I saw below to create new sense from the patterns of the shadows.

Here near the corner of the house were a bush, a wheelbarrow, and a garden hose. I worked with them, finding new meaning in their outlines. I smiled as the snake, the bull, and the goat shifted back to ordinary garden items.

I picked a new section of the yard for my attention and found something that looked like a grape arbor and a flower-covered bush. This, I decided, was the opposite side of the house from the direction of our after-dinner walk. I felt strange about changing shapes, creating new objects, when I wasn't altogether sure of what I was looking at.

As I rested there against the windowsill, I slowly transformed the arbor into a shed and the shed into a playhouse. The bush with its white flowers first became a sheep and then a dog. I could just make out the shape of someone sitting on the doorstep of the playhouse.

I had reached that point—dog, playhouse, person in the doorway—when my vision became "set." It was just like those times when you're looking at one of the optical-illusion drawings and *know* there's a second way to see but can't find it. I couldn't make myself see the alternatives. Suddenly, the things I had invented were all I could see.

Follow one line, I told myself. *Move your eyes along*

the roof of the playhouse until you see the arch of the arbor.

I tried. Over and over, I tried, but I was stuck with the playhouse, the figure in the doorway, and the white dog.

Maybe I had been wrong about the reality. Maybe for once I had started with the illusion. After all, the dog and the building could be the reality, while the bush and the arbor were imaginary.

For better or worse, all I could now see were dog and playhouse. And with every passing moment, I was becoming more convinced that the figure in the doorway was a child. I don't know how long I sat, but I do know I didn't feel even one twinge of fear. After a while I realized that I couldn't fall asleep, that I was not going to fall asleep until I somehow found out what was real in the shadowy forms and lines of the garden.

As soon as I consciously accepted that realization, I slipped out of bed and pulled on the housecoat Mother always insists I take along when we travel. Karen was sound asleep so I left the room as quietly as I could. Because there were tall windows at both ends of the hallway, I was able to find my way to the stairs easily. Without turning on a light or stumbling over anything, I made my way to the outside door and went out into the moonlit night.

I wasn't exactly happy about what I was doing, wandering around a strange yard in the dark, but for the moment I put aside my fears. I *had* to see.

Almost at once I spotted the house I'd seen from my

second-story window. And it *was* a house, a playhouse, though I seemed to be approaching it from the side. I walked around it until I came to its front. I didn't even jump at the sight of the child, a little girl, who was sitting there. I think by then I was sure she would be there.

"Who are you?" I asked softly. She didn't appear to be much older than Karen, and I was certain she had no business sitting out there in the dark and, as I saw now, crying.

She didn't answer me or give any sign that she had heard me.

"Here, don't cry," I said, trying again to capture her attention. I knelt beside her and put my arm around her shoulder. She was so much like Karen that it just seemed natural. "Can you tell me your name?"

"Filly."

"Filly?" I asked, thinking I couldn't have heard right.

She nodded, leaning her head into my shoulder and leaving it there.

"What are you doing here?"

"They think he's mad. They're going to kill him."

"Who?" I had no idea what she was talking about.

"Snowball. They say he has hydrophobia." She said the word syllable by syllable, distinctly and with loathing.

"Who's Snowball?"

"Him." She gestured. What I had at first taken for a "snowball bush" and then for a dog really was a dog, apparently a dog named Snowball.

The dog, as I now clearly saw him to be, was sitting

about ten feet from us and watching us with comparative calm. I say "comparative" because his chest was heaving and even at that distance I could see in the moonlight the white flecks of foam at the corners of his mouth.

"Are—are they sure he has rabies, uh, hydrophobia?" I asked, suddenly thinking that neither of us should be sitting here under the watchful eye of a mad dog.

"He *doesn't*," she said. "He truly doesn't. But today he just went wild, racing and tearing through town and foaming at the mouth. I don't know why he did it, but I know he doesn't have the hydrophobia. I just know it."

It sounded like hydrophobia to me. I watched the dog, assessing the distance and wondering how quickly I could pull the child (Filly?) through the door behind us if the dog moved toward us.

"What will they do with him?"

"The sheriff is coming. Father says half the people in town complained about the mad dog, so the sheriff will have to come and shoot him."

Her head pressed back into my shoulder but no more sobs came.

I thought I heard a noise from the side of the house and turned my head to look in that direction. Looking away almost made me miss the dog's sudden jump. As it was I caught the motion from the corner of my eye. He leaped into the air. I grabbed Filly even tighter, but Snowball wasn't headed our way. He raced across the yard making a white blur in the moonlight and running as if he were being chased by a demon.

"He isn't mad. He isn't," Filly said. "But he keeps running away from me."

"Filly! Filly! Come in now," called a voice from the shadows at the side of the house.

"I have to go," the child said. And, sliding under my arm, she ran off in the direction of the voice.

I took a last look around. I hadn't found what I had expected, but I believed I'd at least found out what was real. I stood up and moved briskly away from the playhouse. With a mad dog running around the garden, I couldn't afford to stay there.

At that moment, the moon disappeared behind the clouds, plunging the garden into darkness. And what a darkness! I couldn't even see vague outlines. I couldn't find so much as a shadow to guide me. I had never been in such complete blackness before. At first, I couldn't move from terror. Besides the mad dog that I knew about, what other horror might not be hidden in that inky blackness?

I moved forward a step at a time, trying not to cry out loud in my fear. Any moment, the light will come back, I told myself. But minutes passed as I made slow progress and the light didn't return. There was no longer even the occasional flicker of a firefly. I felt more isolated, more alone, more frightened than at any other time in my life.

When I stubbed my toe against the back step, I could have cried with relief. I fumbled open the back door, made my way to the stairs, and climbed them to find that in the upper hallway the light of the moon shone brightly through the tall windows once more. Slipping into my room, I climbed into bed a second time, this time resolutely turning my back to the window.

When I woke the next morning, Karen was gone from her bed. I dressed and went down to the kitchen where I found Aunt Lydia stirring up something in a big bowl.

"You've missed the crowd, sleepyhead. But I can still mix you up some pancakes. Or would you rather have French toast?"

"Just plain toast, please. I want to try your blackberry jelly. Dad says it's famous."

"Well, it is good," she said smiling, "but probably not famous."

"Aunt Lydia, do you know a little girl named Filly who has a dog named Snowball?" I asked her.

"Filly and Snowball! Now, where did you hear of them? Filly! For heavens sake, don't let Aunt Phyllis hear you talking about Filly. Why, she hasn't been called that for fifty years and more."

"Aunt Phyllis? I was thinking of some child here in the neighborhood."

"Someone else called Filly? No, I don't think so. We'd know of her. I think you must have heard someone talking about your old aunt. She was young once, you know."

"What about Snowball? Do you know of anyone who has a dog named Snowball?"

"Why, of course I do! That's what made me so sure you had heard something about Phyllis as a little girl.

She used to have a big ol' white spitz named Snowball. I remember the summer he scared us right out of our wits—"

At that moment I began to be pretty scared myself. I felt sure of what was coming next, a story of a dog that had had rabies and been shot more than fifty years ago, a dog that had belonged to a little girl named Filly, who'd sat in a playhouse doorway and cried for her dog.

In self-defense, I cut in on her reminiscences and said, "Did he have rabies?"

"Now I know you've been hearing tales! But here's Phyllis. She'll tell you. Phyllis, you remember your dog Snowball? Meredith is asking about him."

"Snowball? How'd you get hold of that old story?"

"I—I was just asking. Someone must have mentioned him."

Aunt Phyllis settled in at the kitchen table, and her eyes filled with remembered scenes.

"What a scare that was! The poor dog went wild, racing and tearing all over town. People were calling the law and demanding protection from a mad dog. They said he had rabies—hydrophobia we called it then. But I never believed it for a minute. For one whole night I lived in dread knowing that the sheriff would be coming in the morning.

"The next day when he came, he brought his rifle. I can see him right now. An old west marshal, that's what he looked like. He was tall and thin as a rail and he had a cigarette hanging from the corner of his mouth. I got a good look at him and then I ran and hid behind our playhouse. I crouched there and pressed my hands over my ears so I couldn't hear the shot when the sheriff killed Snowball. I waited and waited but nobody ever came to tell me what had happened, so finally I crept out.

"I walked around the house and there I found Mama and the sheriff standing and talking, even laughing. The sheriff saw me and said, 'That's no mad dog, but he sure needs worming. I had my doubts when I heard he was running away from people. Mad dogs don't scare so easily. He just got a case of worms that's driving him wild.'"

"We wormed that dog," Aunt Lydia added, "and he lived another twelve years. Snowball was still here when I went off to college."

"I wonder what made you ask about Snowball," Aunt Phyllis said again.

But I couldn't tell her.

In spite of the good jelly, the toast stuck in my dry throat. When I had choked down the last bite, I stood up to leave. On impulse, I gave each of the aunts a hug and found that Phyllis's thin shoulders felt not much different from those of the little girl the night before.

Of course, before we left, I saw all of the yard by daylight—and found the grape arbor and a snowball bush in full bloom. I didn't even ask about the play-house. I knew it was gone. It had to be. It had stood on the ground the arbor now filled. And two different buildings can't occupy the same space, not when there's daylight to make them more than shadowed outlines.

I shivered in the sunlight thinking how real it had seemed—the little girl, the dog's eyes that gleamed in

A TRICK OF THE LIGHT

the dark, even the flash of white as Snowball had raced away.

That was the last time I played my game of fooling myself with light and shadow. Somehow it doesn't appeal to me anymore. Where was I that night when I stepped out of the house and found Filly and Snowball? And where was I when the light went away? Is it possible to be in between times, to be nowhere at all? I can't help wondering.

These days if the robe hanging on the back of my door begins to look like a person standing there in the doorway, I immediately reach for the lamp switch and restore the room to its own hundred-watt reality.

A
GAME
OF STATUES

"**I** DOAN HAB a code! My doz is 'tuffy. Thad's awd it idz."

It's pathetic, Brian thought, watching the red-haired boy plead with his classmates to let him join their game of storm-the-castle.

"Get lost, Tommy. Nobody wants your 'awd code'!" shouted the one called Mark.

Brian quickly turned away before Tommy could notice him. Better to be on my own than stuck with a creep my first day in a new school, he told himself.

Brian was an old hand at adjusting to new schools. He had moved seven times in the last two years. With all of that experience, he had developed basic rules for settling into a new place. He was never in a hurry to be friendly. He took his time sizing up a class. The important thing was to spot the leader.

It was easy to spot the leader here. Mark was clearly the most powerful boy in the class. You'd never catch Brian begging to join in a game like that drippy Tommy. No, Brian knew a better way. The first couple of days would be tough, but he had learned to be patient. By the end of the week Mark and the rest would be begging to play his game.

Watching from the schoolroom window, Mrs. Whitman shook her head. She saw Tommy Humphreys turn away in dejection. She waited to see if Tommy and the new boy would team up. They didn't. The new boy wasn't trying to join the others' game, she noted. Some of the boys should have asked him. She'd have a private word with Mark after school. Brian appeared content on his own, but the others should have tried to make him feel welcome.

The April afternoon passed slowly in the classroom. Asked to read aloud from *The American Stories Anthology*, Brian read clearly and with no appearance of shyness. When Mrs. Whitman asked Tommy to explain a math problem from the homework assignment, he flushed to the roots of his red hair and said, "I habn't got id done."

A snicker of contempt started from Mark, who held his own nose and said, "He diden hab tibe to do id!" The snicker spread through the class.

It struck Mrs. Whitman as odd that she had never found Mark unpleasant before.

The next day clouds darkened the morning sky. Before the first recess, rain had begun to fall in sheets, lashing the windows and blotting out the world outside.

During the break from their schoolwork, the children played with marbles or jacks in the hall outside the room or stayed at their desks and talked. Except for Brian. Brian sat at his desk reading until class began again.

At lunch Mrs. Whitman spoke to her friend Mrs. Ames, who taught the other fifth-grade class.

"Of course it's hard to tell with a new student. He seems to be adjusting well, but he simply has nothing to do with the others. And since he came," she added, rushing a bit now that she had gotten around to her real worry, "the others seem different."

"How do you mean 'different'?" Marge Ames asked her friend.

"Oh, not as easygoing as they used to be." Somehow she couldn't bring herself to say that the class, which she had liked well enough last week, now seemed to be made up of unpleasant and unlikable children. Except for Brian.

Mrs. Whitman had allowed them thirty minutes to finish filling the blanks in the exercise assigned in their social studies workbook. Brian had finished in seven minutes, but he pretended to continue working, looking up occasionally to study one or another of his classmates. Joey and Harold looked like twins and acted like twin servants to Mark. They weren't really related, Brian knew; but their blond hair combed just alike and their devotion to Mark made them seem like bookends. Brian's glance slid past Tommy, dismissing him as of no importance. Carl was chewing the end of his pencil and staring blankly at his workbook. He wouldn't finish the assignment and it wouldn't matter because everything he did was wrong anyway. The next time Brian looked up he sought out Mike, a serious boy who probably had more brains than Mark but who let himself be led around like a sheep.

Brian sighed and turned a page in his workbook. It was always the same. More than anything he wanted friends; he wanted to be part of it all—the games, the jokes, the roughhousing. And it would work too, if only he could just walk into a school and be one of the gang instantly.

It's the waiting that ruins it, he thought. Once you start to watch them, it's all spoiled. He looked up again and saw Tommy surreptitiously wiping his nose on his shirt sleeve. Brian dreamed of having a boon companion, not a drippy follower who would latch on to him because nobody else would let him play with them.

Just for an instant, he pictured himself balanced on a log over the creek jousting with Mark. Brian shook his head, chasing away the picture. Mark wouldn't do for the kid in his dream any more than Tommy would. Brian's best friend couldn't be a bully, a whiner, a copycat, or a sheep. He scanned the room again, ignoring the girls. No, taking a look at people spoiled them for you. Mrs. Whitman called time, and Brian shrugged. It was okay. He would play with them anyway. Sometime soon.

In a sudden spring chill of the sort that can rise unexpectedly in the northern plains states, the town was gripped with frost that night. And there was talk on the weather report of another snow in the offing. Mrs.

Whitman noted that the spring clothing had been put aside the next day. The children came to school with warm sweaters covered by their heavy jackets. All except Brian.

At recess time, she called him aside to ask if he would be warm enough.

"The cold doesn't bother me," he told her.

"If you feel chilled, you can come and stay in the room. We can't have you out there freezing."

He smiled at her, a fleeting expression that went straight to her heart and made her think again, What a nice child he is!

Mrs. Whitman made up her mind to cut recess short that Wednesday. No sense in letting the kids catch cold. From her vantage point at the classroom window, she watched them. Within minutes, the girls began to return, taking up quiet games inside the building rather than facing winter's last blast. Perhaps I should call them all back in now, Mrs. Whitman thought. But she stopped, her attention caught by the scene outside.

The two opposing teams in storm-the-castle were slowly being killed off. As they "died" in battle, the boys left the game one by one. Today there were several of them wandering around, left out of the final battle. A stupid way to play any game, Brian thought. But in all his various schools, he had had a chance to see lots of different leaders. Letting people drop out of the game was a mistake plenty of leaders made. It was a mistake Mark was making. So far Mark had just ignored Brian. Mark, as the established leader here, was so sure of himself that he was confident the new kid would eventually come to him asking to join a game, if not this one then the next one. Brian knew exactly what was going on in Mark's head. He knew because he had known so many kids like Mark, not that all leaders were alike, but a lot of them were like Mark. He belonged to the "bully-organizer" category of leader, the ones who take charge by pushing people around and always having plenty of ideas of what to do next. He scared them and he kept one step ahead of them. But not ahead of Brian.

Everybody who was not part of Mark's game had gathered in a knot at the edge of the playing field. It was time to make a start, time for Brian to make a move.

"What'll we do?" somebody asked.

"Statues," Brian answered clearly and firmly before discussion could start. "We'll play a game of statues."

For a wonder, nobody bothered to say "That's kidstuff!" In fact, they didn't even seem to know the game. Brian had to explain.

"That's all there is to it," he said, when he had covered the rules. "The way we'll play though is that nobody drops out. If the Master of the Game catches you moving, he'll just cast his eye on you and freeze you. You'll be a statue for the rest of the game."

"What if somebody gets caught but still tries to sneak forward to win?" Joey asked. "I think we ought to put people out when they're caught moving."

"I'll be Master of the Game," Brian said. "Just try moving after I catch you."

"Aw, heck, let's give it a try."

Mark's game of storm-the-castle had used the bleachers beside the playing field as a castle. As the last of the victorious knights straggled back across the field, they were startled to see all the losers from their game spread out over the lower half of the field, some standing poised for movement but holding very still and others seemingly frozen in the middle of motion. Joey had both arms flung out, one knee raised high in the air as though leaping and only one toe touching the ground. He looked as though he would fall over if you tapped him. Carl seemed to have fallen already and was resting on the toes of both feet and the tip of his nose, with his arms raised toward the sky above his back.

Mark and his last surviving knights raced toward them in astonishment. Just before they reached the group, Brian called out, "Game's over. We'll have to play again tomorrow."

"What's going on here?" Mark asked.

Nobody answered him. Harold grabbed Joey's arm. "How could you just freeze like that?"

"I don't know. It felt really strange."

"He didn't catch be," Tommy bragged through his stuffy nose.

But no one was interested in who hadn't been caught.

"When the Master of the Game turned and saw me moving, it felt like ice crystals formed all through me. I couldn't have moved another fraction of an inch," Mike explained.

"Well, I don't know how to describe it, ice crystals or what," Carl said, "but I did feel sort of like a snowman or something."

"Snow*ball*, you mean," Mark said, still trying to take charge of the conversation, but it was too late. They were back at the classroom.

On Thursday, the predicted snow still hadn't come, though the temperature stayed near freezing.

Mrs. Whitman warned, "Let's enjoy outdoor recess while we can. Tomorrow we may have that snowstorm and not be able to get out at all."

This recess all the boys joined the game of statues. Mrs. Whitman watched as the various players tried to creep toward the Master. Mark seemed especially determined; he clearly wanted to win the right to become the Master himself. But Brian was quick. Some of the boys shuffled forward constantly when Brian's back was turned, but he could whirl with astonishing speed and catch them. Some of the boys stood very still and then dashed forward. Brian seemed to sense the very moment they started to move. The strange thing was the way they stopped. Oh, the ones who weren't caught looked normal enough. But, when Brian caught them moving, they froze in midair, holding the pose like real statues.

In spite of herself, Mrs. Whitman felt contempt for the players' clumsy efforts against Brian. She reminded herself that her boys were ordinary students just like the ones in every class she had taught: a pair of friends who wanted to be just alike, a leader who was a bit of a bully, a bright boy who lacked confidence, a stuffy-nosed kid who whined. They were just boys like any others, but something had happened to her sympathy for them.

I'm seeing them from an outsider's point of view, she thought. She looked again at Brian and shivered. The cold, like her new view of her students, seemed to have come with Brian.

When recess ended, no one moved until Brian called an end to the game, with no one having managed to reach him. The boys came in grouped in twos and threes, talking, almost gasping out their sense of adventure, eyes wide with excitement. All except Brian, who came in as quietly as usual.

The game hadn't looked that exciting, but the players seemed to feel they'd had a wild and dangerous outing.

During the afternoon, Mrs. Whitman asked them to write a story, a story with a snowy setting, she specified, eyeing the snow clouds thickening outside. In the last hour of the schoolday, she had the fifth-graders read their stories out loud.

Brian had written a story about a snow king's garden. Purple, gold, and white crocuses pushed through the snow in the king's garden, and every day he went out to admire the flowers, but the flowers begged to be picked and made into a bouquet. Day after day the king refused. Finally, he couldn't resist their pleas. He picked them, put them all together in a bowl, and brought them into his castle. The next day all the flowers had wilted.

As Brian read the chilling story, the listeners felt that they were bright petals, pushing out through a crust of snow to stand trembling under the spring sun.

When Brian finished his story, the class sat silent.

Mrs. Whitman sat silent too, thinking it a strange story for a ten-year-old to write.

Mark snapped out of the spell of the story first. A little angrily, he said, "Snow kings and crocuses! That's dumb!"

Mrs. Whitman stepped in quickly to offer positive comments. Mark had never seemed so rude before these last few days.

Mrs. Whitman was always delayed a few minutes after school was over, straightening the room and preparing for the next day. When she left that afternoon, she was surprised to see that the boys from her class were still outside the building. They appeared to be continuing their game from the morning recess, all of them in staggered lines playing at being statues. All except Brian, who was still the Master of the Game.

She was cooking her supper at home when her phone rang the first time.

"Carl isn't home. Do you know where he can be?" her caller asked.

As soon as she had finished talking to Carl's mother, Joey's mother called.

"Joey didn't come home from school. I've talked to Harold's mother, and he isn't home yet either."

When Mark's father called next, Mrs. Whitman decided that she had better go over to the schoolyard as she had directed the parents to do. During the day when the weather was fair, it was possible to see the field behind the school from her back porch. But now it was night, and a night made even darker by clouds.

As she reached the school grounds, she could hear parents shouting. Just then someone turned on the lights for the playing field, and in the sudden brightness she saw the boys from her class. They were standing still as statues, frozen into the oddest postures. She moved quickly among them, checking them against a mental roll. Yes, they were there, all of them. All except, of course, Brian.

THE
CHILDREN
OF WINTER

D ODGING A FINAL flurry of snowballs, the two Rogers children reached their front porch.

"Come on. Let's get the sled," Kerwin urged, pulling open the door.

"We'll be right back," Kelly yelled to their pursuers. "I have to change clothes," she told Kerwin, scooting through the door behind him.

A huge snowball flattened itself against the glass of the front door.

"I just need my boots," Kerwin told her. "I'll meet you out back."

"Wait for me, okay?" she begged her older brother. "Don't start up the hill without me."

In less than five minutes, Kelly had put on snowpants, a shirt, a heavy sweater, and a woolen hat.

In the kitchen she pulled on her boots, her waterproof jacket, and her gloves; said hi-goodbye to her mother; and raced out the back door to join Kerwin. It was Friday, and the children were free for two whole days.

And, during the day, the first snow of the year—a soft, deep, sledding snow—had fallen.

Kelly's brother had compromised between waiting for her and climbing the hill without her by joining a group of kids at the foot of their sledding hill.

Only one road wound up the hill, at the top of which lay Apple Acres Farm. The road wasn't much used, and the old woman who lived alone at Apple Acres was glad to have children sledding down her hill and into the fields at its base.

"Let's go," a boy named Claude cried as Kelly joined the group.

An odd assortment of sledding gear was spread among the group: Flexible Flyers, round plastic disks, trash can lids, inner tubes, a sheet of metal with one end curled, an ultra-fast sled with steering wheel, and a couple of plastic trash bags. Almost anything worked fine on their sledding hill.

"Do you want to go first?" Kerwin asked when they reached the top.

"You go ahead," Kelly offered, to his relief. "I want to see Mrs. Hobbleberry before I start sledding."

Mrs. Hobbleberry was the owner and sole tenant of Apple Acres Farm, from which she sold eggs and a little butter. The orchards that gave the farm its name had been gone for the past two generations. Now the only apples at Apple Acres came from six or eight trees just outside the barnyard.

Just before she reached the house, Kelly broke into a run to build up momentum for a slide across a patch of ice.

"Halloo, child," a round, red-cheeked woman called from the screen door of the back porch.

"Are they here?" Kelly asked, a little breathless from the climb and the run and slide. "Are they coming today?"

"Heavens, child! Aren't you even going to say hello?"

Kelly gave her a quick hug and a kiss on a wrinkled red-and-white cheek.

"I *am* glad to see you, but I couldn't help thinking about the children. We've been waiting for them all year."

"Come on in and we'll talk about the children. I've missed them too, you know. It has been so quiet around here. When they're here, they do most of the work for me. They gather the eggs and do the milking, feed the animals, bring in firewood. Why, the last time they were here, they painted the bedrooms!"

"Maybe they'll do the kitchen ceiling this year," Kelly said, looking up at the peeling paint high above them.

"Hmm," Mrs. Hobbleberry looked up speculatively, as though she hadn't noticed the ceiling's plight before. "Perhaps they will. I think I'll ask them."

"When? When are they coming?" Kelly asked, not able to wait any longer.

"I just don't know. The snow has come on so suddenly. I've hardly had time to plan."

"Could we help you? I mean, would it spoil anything if we helped you? Wouldn't it be all right? We could start right now."

Kelly wasn't sure Mrs. Hobbleberry had heard her. The cheery face was turned toward the black wood stove, but the blue eyes seemed to be seeing something else altogether. Kelly had the uneasy feeling she might have said something very rude.

At last the clear blue eyes returned to Kelly. "Yes, I do think you all might help."

Mrs. Hobbleberry smiled.

"Instead of 'Too many cooks,'" she continued, "we'll make this a case of 'The more the merrier.'"

"I'll go bring the others."

"Hurry along now. I think I've caught your impatience."

Kelly told Kerwin first; and, because he was older, he took charge, telling all the kids at the top of the hill and sending two of them down on their sleds to tell the children at the bottom of the hill that they were all going to help Mrs. Hobbleberry get ready for her winter visitors.

"She's a witch," Steven Slade said.

"She is not," Kelly said hotly.

Ramona Fisk, who was just coming up the hill, overheard them. "She can't be a witch. My dad says milk always goes sour around a witch. Sometimes Mrs. Hobbleberry sells sweet cream and butter along with her eggs. If she was a witch, the cream would be sour."

"Would you be scared of her if she was a witch?" Kerwin asked Steven.

"Nah, not me."

"Then it doesn't matter. Come on. Let's go."

Fourteen children trooped into the farmhouse at the top of the hill, all of them covered with a dusting of snow and filled with a wish to see some magic before the afternoon was through.

Mrs. Hobbleberry hadn't wasted a moment since Kelly left. She had set out mixing bowls along the kitchen table and laid out aprons and long wooden spoons. As soon as they came in, she gave Kerwin and Claude huge bowls and sent them to bring up flour from the cellar. She stationed three of the girls beside the bowls, each with a different recipe. The rest of the children were given dustpans, brooms, and mops and led away to "get the bedrooms ready."

Mrs. Hobbleberry herself was kept busy seeing that everyone was doing his part. To speed them along in their work, she taught the cleaners a song that began "Above, about, and around, while snow lies on the ground" and ended in a rousing chorus of "Cittery, cattery, coo, dithery, dathery doo." The tune kept the workers moving briskly with brooms and dusters.

To the cooks in the kitchen, she taught, "Before, beside, behind, we'll cook with thoughts so kind." This one too ended with a chorus of "Cittery, cattery, coo . . ."

When the dough began to get stiff and difficult for the girls to stir, Mrs. Hobbleberry put three older boys in their places and sent the girls to "see to the chickens." The cows fell to the lot of Kerwin and Claude, who had helped with this chore before and knew just what to do.

When the house was clean and the animals cared for and tubs of dough set to rise, Mrs. Hobbleberry led all the children into the yard to build the snow people. The children knew that the snow people were part of the magic and had to be built just right.

"Three," Mrs. Hobbleberry insisted. "Three is always the best number." And she gave them a new verse to sing:

Hobbleberry, shobbleberry, stuffleberry, stew.
We're working a magic to make them come true.
We'll shape them and stuff them and fill them with
*   fun.*
We'll give them strong arms to get the work done.
Hobbleberry, chobbleberry, chuckleberry, chew.
Shackleberry, shumbleberry, humbleberry, boo!

Everyone was rolling snowballs, trying for good, round, solid ones to make the snow people strong, when Mrs. Hobbleberry exclaimed, "There's no sugar! I have no sugar at all, and we must have a bit to mix with the snow."

Because she and Kerwin lived closest to Apple Acres, Kelly volunteered to go home for sugar. She rode the sled from the top of the hill and practically sailed into her own backyard.

"Mother!" she called as she burst through the back door. "Can I have some sugar for Mrs. Hobbleberry? She needs it for the snowmen."

"Are all the children helping her?" Kelly's mother asked, as she opened the cupboard.

"Yes, yes," Kelly said, full of the excitement from the top of the hill. "Does she really work magic? Steven said she's a witch."

"Mrs. Hobbleberry has been living alone at Apple Acres for as long as I can remember. She was here when I was a child," Mrs. Rogers said, bringing out a ten-pound bag of sugar. "She's not a witch, but she has a bit of magic of her own." The very last words were said to an empty kitchen.

Clutching the big sack and calling goodbye, Kelly was already out the door. She put the sack of sugar on the sled and pulled it up the hill.

"So much sugar!" Mrs. Hobbleberry said when she saw the sack. "We just need a sprinkle for the snowmen. Perhaps we can make some nutbreads and cakes. The children are always hungry when they get here."

When the three snow people—lightly sprinkled with sugar for a bit of sweetness—were completed, the helpers dressed them, choosing from a stack of coats, dresses, aprons, mufflers, sweaters, mittens, shoes. Mrs. Hobbleberry insisted on the mittens and shoes.

"They're not a bit of good without hands and feet. And there's so much to be done!"

When the work was finished to everyone's satisfaction (two snowgirls and one snowboy), the group went back into the house for hot chocolate.

The bread dough was shaped into loaves and popped into the oven of the old black iron stove that both heated the kitchen and cooked the food.

"Come back in the morning," Mrs. Hobbleberry told everyone as they left. "The children should be here by then."

Most of the children chattered excitedly on the way home, though Kelly noticed that Kerwin was quiet. Just outside their own door, she asked, "It is true, isn't it Kerwin? The children will come?"

He didn't answer her directly.

"That kitchen ceiling is in bad shape. I think it ought to be this year's project."

"So the children have to come, don't they?"

That evening Kelly talked to her mother again about Mrs. Hobbleberry.

"She told us how she never had children of her own and that gave her the idea of making snow children. She said she does it for the love of the children's company, but she's glad of the help with chores. She says they do all the things her real children would do for her if she had any. Do you think I'll really see them this year?"

"You saw them today, didn't you? You even helped to build them."

"Just snowmen, not real, not come to life. Mrs. Hobbleberry says they're wonderful sledders and that, if they come to life tonight, they may slide right down the hill first thing and knock on our door in the morning."

Kelly fell asleep that night thinking of all the things she had ever heard about Mrs. Hobbleberry's children. They were supposed to be great friends to the other children, sliding down the hill on their snow bellies with as many as three children on their backs. All day long they helped Mrs. Hobbleberry while other children went to school and then in the afternoons they played and made snow games more fun than they had ever been before. She imagined the wind whistling past as she flew down the hill on a feathery-soft snowperson.

The knock on her back door came just as she finished breakfast the next morning. Kelly flew out of her chair and swung the door wide in spite of the cold blast of outside air.

Her face fell with disappointment when she saw Ramona and Bobby.

"We want to go to Mrs. Hobbleberry's to see if the children are here yet. Come with us."

"Come in while I get my coat and boots."

Kelly called Kerwin, found her coat, and came back to hear Ramona and Bobby and her mother talking about Mrs. Hobbleberry.

"When I was a little girl," her mother was saying, "Mrs. Hobbleberry used to say, 'I'm not a witch, nor yet a fairy. I'm just a plain old Hobbleberry.' Every year she has new rhymes and a new bit of magic."

"But is it real?" Ramona asked.

"Well," Mrs. Rogers replied, "she claims her children do her work all winter while her arthritis is so bad that she can't manage for herself. And I know for a fact that every winter since I was younger than you her work has been taken care of, year after year."

The four children set off together up the hill and soon reached Mrs. Hobbleberry's back door, passing the trio of gaily dressed snowmen.

"They aren't here," Mrs. Hobbleberry said. "Or rather, they're still *there*." She pointed to the snow people standing just as they'd stood yesterday. "But do come in."

Inside the house the girls got started on making nut breads. After a few minutes, Bobby and Kerwin went out to begin bringing the winter supply of wood from the yard onto the back porch. Before long they were joined by half a dozen helpers and several other children had wandered into the kitchen to help chop dates and nuts.

"We're making plenty of food for them, aren't we?" asked seven-year-old Rebecca.

"Why do you think they haven't come?" Ramona asked Mrs. Hobbleberry.

Mrs. Hobbleberry paused because the group who had moved the wood were now traipsing into the kitchen. When everyone was present, Mrs. Hobbleberry said, looking as sad as such a naturally happy person could look, "I'm afraid I said too much about all the work to be done. They're always such good workers that I just didn't stop to think. I may have frightened them away."

"How about if we help with the work? We'll get most of it done before they come!"

"Yes, we'll work so they can play for all of this winter!"

"We're just as good workers as the snow children."

As soon as all the baking was safely out of the way, carefully stored up against all the cold weeks to come, the boys brought in two tall ladders and took turns scraping the old paint off the kitchen ceiling.

"What can the rest of us do?" Kelly asked.

"Well, let me see." Mrs. Hobbleberry thought hard for a moment. "There's all my mending to be done. My fingers are too stiff, and the snow girls are never any good at that. Their fingers are too big and clumsy."

"We'll do it. We can do it better," the girls chorused.

All morning the crowd of children worked and sang and scraped and painted. The younger children found that not only were they allowed to join in but they were expected to help. If stitches were loose or paint strokes weren't smooth, nobody said, "Here, stupid, let me."

The work wasn't finished on that one Saturday, but the children left with a promise to keep coming back until everything was done.

As they walked toward the hill, Bobby raced past Kelly and Kerwin and shouted, "Her old snow children may have let her down, but we won't. We're not afraid of a little work!"

"What's the truth?" Kelly asked her older brother when Bobby disappeared over the edge of the hill. "If there aren't really any snow children, why do people like to fool us and pretend there are?"

"If they weren't real, wouldn't you like to pretend anyway?"

"No! I want to see them," Kelly cried.

"They're here," Kerwin told her. "Just look around."

They had reached the top of the big slope that led to their own back door. A new snow had begun to fall, clinging to dark jackets like powdered sugar on gingerbread men. Kelly peered through the falling snow, but all she could see were the children, all the helpers from Mrs. Hobbleberry's house, laughing and happy.

"You mean us, don't you? We're Mrs. Hobbleberry's snow children."

Kerwin grinned. "Right now we are, but her children have been coming to help for twenty years. Somehow or other they always show up."

Kelly wasn't sure if she felt pleased or disappointed or maybe proud. She'd have to think about it.

"Climb on my back," Kerwin urged. "The snow's perfect."

Her brother flopped onto the sled, and Kelly climbed on top of him. The double weight sent the sled flying like magic over the frosted length of the hill.

THE
FIRESIDE BOOK
OF GHOST STORIES

T HE PACKAGE was wrapped in red and white foil
with a pair of candy canes stuck on like crossed
swords. I'd saved it for near the end because I expected
something special; but, when the wrapping fell away, I
felt a stab of disappointment. Uncle Jonathan had finally slipped.

Did you ever notice how each year your favorite present seems to come from the same person? In my case it's
my Uncle Jonathan. I hardly ever see him, but at
Christmas and on my birthday each year his presents
arrive. All my life he has seemed to know what I wanted
before I knew myself. The toy dalmatian he sent when I
was four was the stuffed toy I dragged around all day and
took to bed with me at night. Then the year my mother
said "no guns," Uncle Jonathan sent me a space gun.
He gave me a set of knights in armor and a toy sword.
He had even sent some good books: *Captain Blood,
Kim, Tom Sawyer*. But the book inside the package with
the candy canes was a thick, old, tan volume that
looked as though it had been dropped in a mud puddle.

The lower half of the book was swollen from having been wet. The cover was mildewed, and the pages had water stains running halfway up. The spine was torn. It didn't look like the kind of thing I'd have given to anybody, especially not a favorite nephew at Christmas. Maybe he'd decided I wasn't worth it any more. Or maybe he'd gotten out of touch with people my age.

I was into electronics that year. Everything I had asked for was high-tech, new, shiny, and complicated. A book of stories—an old, beat-up book—was the last thing I wanted.

I put the book aside without even reading its title, which was practically worn off anyway.

Later that afternoon Uncle Jonathan called to wish us Merry Christmas. When it was my turn to speak to him, he said, "Nathan! What did you think of the book?" Then without giving me a chance to answer, he went on, "I got it when I was twelve, so I figured you'd be about the right age. That was always one of my favorites. Treat it well."

I mumbled and stumbled over thanking him. Treat it well? It didn't look as though he'd treated it very well himself. As soon as I was off the phone I headed back to the tree, scrabbled among the paper and pulled out the book. I might not want it, but it had been embarrassing not even to know the title of the book he'd sent. And he'd said it was one of his favorites, so he had meant well.

As I opened it, a sheet of paper fell out. I retrieved the fallen paper with one hand while I read the title: *The Fireside Book of Ghost Stories*. Ghost stories?

I unfolded the sheet of paper that fallen from the book and found that it was a letter from my uncle:

Dear Nathan,

I was about your age when I got this book. (Incidentally, it wasn't new then. You'll notice it was published in the 1940s.) I hadn't believed in ghosts for several years by that time. This book changed my mind. You see, it isn't just about hauntings; it is haunted.

I know how that sounds, but you'll see what I mean. Or, maybe you won't. Either way you'll have some good, classic ghost stories to read.

I say the book is haunted because of a story that used to be there and then suddenly wasn't there any longer. Besides the disappearing story, it always seemed to me that I couldn't choose what I would read from this book. I've only been able to read what the book would let me find.

At six hundred pages, it's too long to read at one sitting, even if you could take that much horror at once. Also, there are more than forty stories listed in the table of contents. I know people would say with so many stories, it was perfectly natural that sometimes a kid wouldn't be able to find a particular one. Let them say what they will; I know what I know.

Don't take my word for it. Read it for yourself.

> *Best,*
> *Uncle Jon*

After that letter, nothing could have kept me from reading a little of *The Fireside Book of Ghost Stories* that very afternoon. I can't say I noticed anything strange about the book, apart from its graveyard smell of mildew, but the two stories I read were spine-chillers.

The first one was called "The Room in the Tower," a scary story where the horror kept building each time you read the words "Jack will show you to your room. I have given you the room in the tower." The words are from a nightmare, and the reader knows that someday the narrator is going to hear them in reality. That was a good story.

The only other one I read on Christmas day was called "Murder Will Out," a really old story from *The Canterbury Tales*. I just read it because it was short, not expecting to like it much. But things like "thou art" and "revealest" didn't bother me. That one was pretty good too.

Uncle Jonathan was right about one thing. Nobody would read forty or so stories like that all at once. So I put the book on my shelf and over the months I'd pick it up and read a story once in a while. I wouldn't have admitted it at the time but I never read that book in bed at night. I read the ghost stories on Saturdays or when I got home in the afternoons. They just weren't the kind of thing you want to have in mind when you're trying to fall asleep in the dark.

I guess it would be true to say I came to like that book. It hadn't made much of a first impression with its stained pages and moldy smell. But I was still reading the book when I had forgotten about most of the other presents from that Christmas.

I also found that I would pick the book up intending to reread one story and end up reading something entirely different. Unlike my uncle, I didn't attribute that to any sort of magic. Some of the stories' names weren't very memorable. I'd try out two or three possibilities and then, not finding the one I was looking for, settle in to read something else. It wasn't supernatural. I mean the book wasn't hiding the story I was looking for or forcing me to read another one.

For instance, one tale was about a room haunted by the spirit of a wicked old woman whose heirs had turned her mansion into a boarding house. At first, the heirs, who reminded me of the brother and sisters in *Arsenic and Old Lace*, were unaware of the evil in the house. Then they found that none of the boarders would stay in one particular room. The sister who did the cleaning began to get scared to go into the room.

Finally, the sister who did the cooking said she'd move into the room herself. I liked that story because things turned out fine for the sisters and their brother but what happened in between was as scary as anything I've ever read.

Somehow, I could never quite remember the name of that one, so I'd end up looking up anything that had "room" in the title. Naturally, I could never find it when I was deliberately looking for it because the word "room" isn't in the title at all. I figured I had discovered the secret of Uncle Jonathan's "haunted book": Stories didn't disappear; they were hard to find because of their forgettable titles.

I read that book off and on for more than a year. Then midway through my thirteenth year, I put it away and forgot it.

When Uncle Jonathan came to visit us soon after I turned fifteen, I remembered the book again. I asked him what his "disappearing" story had been about.

He glanced at me sharply. Then he grinned and shook his head.

"I'll tell you about it someday. Not now."

That was all I could get out of him. But once again I got out *The Fireside Book of Ghost Stories* and began to read it.

My best friend is Tom McHenry, who's on the swim team with me. That summer we were finally old enough to qualify as counselors at a local camp. I know how popular ghost stories are at camp, so I packed up Uncle Jonathan's book to take along with me.

Sure enough we fell into the habit of telling ghost stories, mostly silly but still scary ones with lots of dramatic effects, to the kids around the campfire. The stories we were telling were nothing like the ones in my book, but they prompted me and Tom to discuss ghost stories in general. We discovered we'd both read quite a few. I offered to let Tom read some of *The Fireside Book of Ghost Stories*.

"Have you ever read this one, the one called 'Friends'?" he asked one day.

I didn't remember the title, so I took the book to read the beginning of the story. I didn't recognize it, but it caught my interest, and I read the whole thing through.

The story was about two friends called Nicholas and Arthur, who lived in Victorian England. The story took place around Christmastime. Although there was ice covering the river behind Arthur's house, the boys had been forbidden to skate on it because it was still thin in spots.

Not long before Christmas, the two went out with a wooden sled to cut holly. When the sled was loaded, they agreed to put on their skates (which they just happened to have brought with them) and skated home along the frozen river pulling the sled.

About halfway home, they skated over a thin patch of ice that broke when the heavy sled was pulled over it. The sled went through the ice, pulling Nicholas down with it. But Arthur managed to escape. He scrambled out into the nearest bank and looked about for an old fence rail, the limb of a tree, anything he could safely extend to his friend. While he searched, Nicholas disappeared beneath the water. Certain that he no longer had a hope of saving Nicholas, Arthur removed his skates and hid them. He then went home and told his father about the accident, claiming that Nicholas had insisted on pulling the sled along the river but that he, Arthur, had refused to go out onto the ice and had followed along on the bank. The grief-stricken families, his own and Nicholas's, believed his story and praised him for doing the right thing.

Then, on Christmas morning, Arthur was found dead in his bed, his body encased in ice.

"Not the sort of story we can tell our campers," Tom

said, laughing, when he saw I had finished reading. "The kids would rather have escaped lunatics and hatchet murders."

It seemed odd that I had never seen the story before, but I figured there must be half a dozen or more stories in the book that I had never read. Still, the gruesome tale drew me, and I read it several times over the next few weeks.

I read it too often. That story got into my dreams. Like a refrain, the same words would show up in dream after dream: "It wasn't my fault. It's too late to save him." Like those nightmare words about Jack showing the way to the tower, those sentences were enough to start me trembling. In my dreams, instead of Arthur and Nicholas, Tom and I were the main characters. There were dark, swirling waters and Tom would slip out of sight each time I tried to reach him.

I'd wake up scared half to death and have to lie there telling myself that Tom is as good a swimmer as I am.

By daylight I'd think the dreams were stupid, but at night I'd break into a sweat of fear.

One night while I was once again dreaming of trying to rescue Tom from murky waters, I seemed to feel my sweat turning to specks of ice all over me. I woke up terrified.

I looked carefully around the cabin where ten boys were also sleeping, counted them to make sure everyone was safe and then checked Tom's bunk. He was there, sleeping peacefully.

The following day I wrote to Uncle Jonathan and asked him again if he'd tell me the story of his own strange experience with *The Fireside Book of Ghost Stories*. It seemed to me that the story "Friends" was haunting my dreams, and I hoped my uncle would say something that would help. I addressed and stamped the letter and dropped it into the mailbox where the campers posted their letters to parents. But, as soon as the letter was through the slot, I was sorry I'd sent it. Uncle Jonathan would think I was some sort of idiot not to have known he was joking. I shrugged and hoped he wouldn't take my letter seriously.

Night after night the dreams continued and I continued to wake up and check the people in my cabin. About a week later I woke up in the middle of an especially hot night. Out of habit, I checked the cabin. The first thing I saw was that Tom was gone, probably outside cooling off. As usual, I checked each bed and saw the boys sleeping—more restlessly than peacefully but at least sleeping. And then I saw that one camper's bunk was empty.

I slipped soundlessly out of bed and out of the cabin. In the moonlight, I saw no one but thought I heard noises from down the hillside.

I plowed straight down the cliff for a few yards. Then I cut through a narrow crevice, clambered over tumbled rocks at the foot of the hill and looked out over a natural pool with a foot-bruising rocky edge. This pond was off-limits for campers who had the use of a chlorinated, olympic-sized pool at the campsite, as well as a lake higher up in the hills.

"Tom!" I called as I saw him pulling himself up onto the rocks from the water.

"Let's go," he said as soon as he was out of the water. "We have to get back before anyone misses us. Just forget we ever came out."

"What are you talking about? What happened? Do you know that one of the campers is missing? That kid Mitchell is not in the cabin."

"I know. He's in there." Tom gestured with a dripping hand toward the pool. "I trailed him down here and saw him dive in. He must have hit his head. It's pretty shallow and there're rocks everywhere. Anyway, he didn't come up. I've dived and dived, but I can't find him. It wasn't my fault. It's too late to save him."

His words knocked the wind out of me like a fist into my solar plexus. The nightmare feeling closed around me.

I seemed to be about three feet above the scene, watching with frozen disinterest. Tom was still talking. But I couldn't hear him. I wasn't thinking. I just acted. My body arced into the air, and I didn't give a thought to the rocks just below the surface. In a shallow dive I cut into the water that was as cold as a river in winter.

When I plunged under the surface, body and awareness merged. Just as I'd done over and over in my dreams, I went searching beneath black waters. I stayed under, feeling among the rocks in a world where sight was useless, until I thought my lungs would burst.

I would have to go up for air.

Just as I was ready to push for the surface, my foot touched something that was not rock. I'd found Mitchell.

I grabbed, pulled, lifted, took a secure hold and struck out for the rocky shoreline.

At the water's edge, Tom met me and between us we lifted Mitchell over the rocks to a leaf-covered patch of ground where we fell to work reviving him. Long seconds passed and stretched into minutes. Tom, ashamed at having quit too soon, pushed me aside and took over. Driven by nightmare-horror on my part and shame on his, neither was going to quit too soon this time. On and on, we tried. And then, Mitchell coughed and at last began to breathe.

Two days later I got a three-page letter from Uncle Jonathan, who hadn't laughed at my request. When he was sixteen, he wrote, he had read and reread a story in *The Fireside Book of Ghost Stories* about a boy whose meetings with a ghost prepare him for his father's death.

After summarizing the story, Uncle Jonathan said:

I seemed to get into that story and live it. And the story got into my dreams. I felt that I knew the characters. When the boy in the story finally learned to accept pain and death and go on living, I learned it too. I had read stories before that meant something to me. I'd even picked up a lesson or two from things I'd read, but this was the first time a story had so much impact that it changed me.

I remembered the name of the story as "Destiny" but in later years when I went back to find it, there was no story of that title listed. I figured I'd gotten the name wrong, so I eventually read through the whole book looking for the story. I never found it again. But that search was much later, long after my sixteenth year, after I no longer needed the story.

The months when I read and reread the story were the months just before my mother died. I think I accepted my own grief with more maturity because through that haunted book I had already known what it was like to lose a parent.

I folded the letter, put it back into its envelope, and went to find *The Fireside Book of Ghost Stories.* No such story as "Destiny" was listed. For curiosity's sake, I went back to the beginning of the list of forty-one titles and looked for "Friends."

I went through it once and then again. No story in the book was called "Friends." One story was called "Playmates," but it was about a lonely little girl who finds ghostly playmates to keep her company. Arthur and Nicholas and the sled loaded with holly weren't any part of it.

I tried all the more likely titles without finding it. Then I asked Tom about the story since he'd been the one to read it first. But he shrugged and said he didn't remember.

I'm still searching. It has to be there: *The Fireside Book of Ghost Stories* was the only book I had at camp.

A PLAGUE
OF CROWDERS OR,
BIRDS OF A FEATHER

"LOOK, MRS. NELLOP, I'm not responsible."

"No," she said thoughtfully and quite seriously, "I daresay not. I've now taught five members of your family and it's my considered opinion that there isn't a *responsible* person among the lot of you."

Mrs. Nellop picked up the wastebasket and swept the broken flowerpot—plant, dirt, and all—into it. It might very well be that Jeff Crowder had had nothing to do with dropping the potted plant onto her desk. But, even if he hadn't done it himself, his actions had probably inspired it.

For almost a decade she had had Crowders in her history classes. Since she taught world history to the eleventh-graders and American history to the twelfth-graders and since the Crowders' sons were spaced at two-year intervals, she hadn't been free of them for a single year. But she was ready for this one, the fifth and last of the lot.

Mrs. Nellop had been the librarian until Cal Crowder, the oldest of the Crowders, had broken a desk over the head of Mr. Bain, the history teacher who had been attempting to explain Grattan's Parliament to his class.

It had been Mrs. Nellop's opinion that Cal Crowder should have been deported, possibly to Antarctica. But Mr. Cordwainer, the principal of the school, had said, "Boys will be boys." And then he'd added, "The war, you know . . ."

No, Mrs. Nellop did not know. "Just how am I expected to deal with boys who have already driven three male teachers away this year?"

"It's the opinion of the board," Mr. Cordwainer said, sheltering behind the Board of Education, "that you are the very best person for this job. If anyone can restore peace and order to the history class, it will be you. We're counting on you, Mrs. Nellop."

That, of course, had happened a little less than ten years ago, and she had brought order to the classroom, though no one else had ever quite appreciated the price she had paid for that quiet, orderly room.

She had taken over classes in which students had known nothing—actually less than nothing because the things they thought they knew were all wrong. She still had some of those first tests she had administered. Five students had written essays about something called the "Silver War" that Americans had fought against the British over the taxes on cotton.

The students had learned nothing from those three teachers who had left battered, physically and mentally. They had learned nothing because until the advent of

Mrs. Nellop the history classes had been chaos.

"Where'd you get those shoes? I bet my dad would like a pair like that."

Those had been the first words Cal Crowder had said to her, earning him a quick laugh from the rest of the class.

Mrs. Nellop had responded to the challenge by taking the class step by step through the formation of the Irish parliament and then assigning them an essay for the following day.

When Cal told her the next morning that he hadn't written an essay, she asked him to substitute an on-the-spot oral report.

With ladylike but biting sarcasm, she then reduced him to a laughingstock.

"You made a fool of me," he told her with quiet rage after the class.

"I thought you enjoyed a good joke, Cal, and your knowledge of history is certainly a joke."

At five feet, one-and-a-half inches, Mrs. Nellop would never be physically imposing. But within a matter of weeks she had gained complete ascendency over her classes. Her sharp wit and even the quirk of her eyebrow were to be feared.

She had a way of ducking her chin and raising her eyebrows while staring unblinkingly at anyone whose word or deed fell below her standards. That tilt-and-stare action turned a spotlight on misbehavior or ignorance. Her look was fearsome. Her disapproval was terrifying.

Mr. Cordwainer and the board gratefully acknowledged that they had found a teacher who could "handle the problem students."

Observing the history classes, it was even possible to sympathize with the students. But that was only half the picture. Midway of that first year, Mrs. Nellop had opened her door one Saturday morning to admit her cat Boswell. Boswell, however, had not been there to come pushing past her, brushing against her legs, meowing to be fed. Mrs. Nellop had looked around. She hadn't looked far before she found Boswell, quite cold and dead, left lying on her steps. He had been shot.

Mrs. Nellop did not mention the matter to anyone. She didn't need to ask who had done the deed. She simply stored it away as over the next few years she would store away many things.

After Cal there had come Warren, Ted, and Martin, each one inspiring new outbreaks of classroom insolence. Mrs. Nellop had mastered them all, had even taught them all a little history. She had not, however, been able to affect their characters.

After Boswell, she had not taken another pet, feeling that it wouldn't be fair to the animal, who might suffer a similar fate. The lack of pets hadn't deterred the Crowders. They had found other ways to plague her. Garbage was strewn across her front porch. Poison added to a birdbath had left her a yard full of dead birds. Once she had been prepared to leave for church when she found that her front door was blocked with rats and mice, all dead and many with the traps still attached. A plague of Crowders, that was how she thought of the Crowder boys.

Mrs. Nellop knew that the more harm you do to a person the more you're inclined to despise that person. She was therefore fully aware that she was heartily abhorred by all the Crowders, who had been doing her harm and hating her for it for years.

"There's hope for every boy," Mr. Cordwainer would tell her from time to time. "They'll turn out to be fine young men. You'll see."

Mrs. Nellop had seen. She had followed the progress of all her former students and the Crowders were a bad lot. So far they had turned out to be loafers, layabouts, and troublemakers—when they found the energy for it.

The Crowders never forgot an imagined injury. So that when Cal had graduated and been replaced by Warren, Cal and Warren had teamed up to plague her. When Ted became her student, he in turn was aided by both Cal and Warren in his efforts to harass her. Keeping track of the Crowders had never been a problem. Their interest in her had been cumulative. Now, this year, she had all five to face.

Fortunately, from Mrs. Nellop's point of view, the Crowders were predictable and gullible as well, which had allowed her to take some defensive action over the years. Their major campaign against her each year always came on April Fools' Day. By the time Ted, the third of the Crowders, had come along, Mrs. Nellop had begun to find ways to direct their malice. Near the end of March that year, she had hired someone to dig a flower bed two feet wide and the full length of her front lawn. She then began to speak loudly and frequently at school about the rare and expensive bulbs that would soon be springing up in her yard. The ruse had worked. The Crowders had dug up her entire front yard, sifting through the dirt for bulbs. The rock garden in her back-yard where she had in fact planted new bulbs was completely unharmed. Planted the autumn before, wild Asian tulips bloomed profusely among the stones. She reseeded the front lawn.

But such minor evasions were both inadequate and unsatisfactory. Mrs. Nellop was always aware when it came to the Crowder boys she was not living up to her own expectations of herself as a teacher.

During a long and busy lifetime, Mrs. Nellop had managed quite a few small miracles of transformation: churning cream into butter, turning lye and fats into soap, and changing curds and whey into cheese. Occasionally, she had even created a silky pursuer of knowledge out of a pigheaded teenager. But try as she might she could not make a decent human being out of a Crowder.

It was true, however, that any number of common transformations involve ingredients that in themselves aren't nice. It isn't pleasant, for example, to think that rennet, which is used in making cheese, is really part of a calf's fourth stomach.

And so, Mrs. Nellop began to think that if such not-too-pleasant ingredients as lye and fat—she always strained out all the impurities but fat was *fat*—could be made into pure, cleansing soap, then perhaps the even less attractive Crowders might have the potential to become something else. She had made it her work to find a formula and to search out just the right additional ingredients to bring about the transformation.

The formula had been found only after years of searching. (Mrs. Nellop took her responsibilities as a teacher very seriously.) It was so old that it was called a "receipt," which is an old-fashioned spelling of "recipe." Still, Mrs. Nellop told herself, a formula for a successful transformation would be as sweet whatever name it might be called.

Then the preparations had taken more than a year. She had found herself hunting down a number of very odd things, hairs from the underbelly of a nursing sow, for instance. Neatly clipped, bottled, and labeled "Bristle," the hairs achieved a sort of dignity. Forty-three ingredients in all she had collected, only having to guess at one or two of them. (She hadn't been at all sure what the Palimenox plant was, for example.) Some, of course, had required additional treatment after they had been found. She had pickled turtles' eggs. soured rabbit's milk, toasted nasturtium seeds.

But finally in March of the last year of the Crowders, she was ready to deal with them. As she had done with some previous success, she began to direct attention toward a particular focus for mischief. One by one, she brought small, heavy crates into her classroom, depositing them with an air of eager anticipation.

"What a treat we'll have next month!" she'd say.

"What is it, Mrs. Nellop?"

"You must wait and see," she told her classes, making

sure Jeff Crowder heard. "We must be sure to keep all these things safe and *separate* from each other until next month. Oh, if they should be mixed, what a disappointment that would be!"

The last of the boxes was added to the collection on March 31, and Mrs. Nellop surveyed the stack with satisfaction. She had done her best. She had made sure everything necessary was available. The rest was up to the Crowders. A teacher, after all, can only do so much. The last step must always be taken by the students.

With good fortune that seemed more than fortuitous, April first fell on a Saturday, allowing both time and freedom to those who wished to play elaborate April Fool's jokes.

When Mrs. Nellop arrived at school the following Monday, she found that someone had broken into her classroom. To the group of students in the hall, she appeared very calm. If anything, she was almost smiling.

She pushed against the door in its splintered jamb and stood for a moment gazing into the room. Every one of those sturdy little crates had been smashed. At first glance all the onlookers saw were the shattered remains of the cases. Next, they noticed that in one corner of the room the desks had been pushed back to make space for an old bathtub that had clearly been brought there for the purpose of mixing together all the contents of those numerous separate packages.

Only at the very last, after all the wreckage had been noted, did someone catch sight of the large black bird perched above the chalkboard—and above the window another, on top of the roll-up maps another, above the door through which students now crowded another, and on the bookcase at the back of the room a fifth one.

"Crows?" Mrs. Nellop said wonderingly. "How surprising. I wonder if the pickled eggs had gone bad?"

She asked some of the students to open the windows and shoo the birds out, which proved difficult and time-consuming. But at last the five birds were outside, scattered among the still-bare branches of a tree, staring in at the students who stood at the windows staring back.

"Who do you think did this?" someone asked.

And someone else gave the obvious answer, which seemed confirmed when Jeff Crowder failed to show up for classes that day.

In the following days he continued to stay away and the rumor slowly spread that all the Crowder sons had left town.

"Unexpected," commented Mrs. Nellop, "but not unsatisfactory." And everyone assumed she was referring to the sudden departure of the town's troublesome boys.

Of course, the thing hadn't turned out precisely as she had intended. A fault in that old "receipt," perhaps? Some inaccuracy in her measurement of ingredients? Or, more likely something in the composition of the Crowders that she had failed to take into consideration. Well, in any case, she couldn't count it a failure.

It is a primary duty of a teacher to help her students become productive citizens of the world. If it is impossible to turn some of them into worthy citizens, then perhaps useful denizens of the air is not a bad alternative.

Unpleasant though crows may be, no one would deny that they do serve a purpose in nature's scheme of things.

These days Mrs. Nellop often steps out her front door to see five haughty crows ranged among the topmost branches of the fir tree in her front yard waiting, as crows do, for a chance to apply themselves to clearing away the remains of any animals unfortunate enough to fall victim to the day's highway traffic.

Mrs. Nellop always nods to them pleasantly and sets briskly off to another day of remolding this year's flock of students.

TAKE
YOUR BEST SHOT

W|ILLIS STRUM was shot during a brief skirmish on March 12, 1864. With a dozen other Confederates, Willis had been caught by a small band of Union soldiers. He had been hit twice and left for dead on the brown, wet leaves under an oak. For a little while, even Willis wasn't sure whether he was dead or alive.

After a bit, he opened his eyes and saw sunlight playing through oak leaves. He had done nothing more than think about moving and test a muscle or two before he knew he couldn't go anywhere without help. He was weak from shock and loss of blood and he'd also had a bone broken by a musketball. But Willis was just nineteen and not so worn down by sickness and short rations as most of the Southern troops were in that spring of '64. He'd be all right if help came soon enough.

He dozed for a time. When he opened his eyes, the sun was directly overhead. Light caught a single drop of water ready to fall from the point of a leaf and, to

Willis's eyes, transformed the drop into a small marble globe that burned with an inner life.

"It's my shooter!" Willis cried, and he wasn't referring to his gun.

The light of the sun directly above him seemed to spread into a rainbow-colored circle and then to break into a hundred different colored dots.

March was usually the time for their first marble games of the year, played in a ten-foot circle on a dry patch of Virginia earth. Instead of fading in the sunlight, the sight of that circle was becoming sharper for Willis. He and Bucky Webber had put their best marbles into the ring, thirteen marbles; mibs and hoodles they called them.

"Bucky'll win," somebody said.

Willis was good too, but somehow everybody always favored Bucky.

The two of them knelt at the pitch line, a line drawn outside the big circle with its center touching the circle, and lagged for the right to shoot first. The lag line was drawn on the opposite side of the circle, also just outside with its center touching the circle. Lagging just meant shooting to come as close to the lag line as possible; the one who shot closest would go first.

"Wait a minute!" Jimmy Johnson cried. "I'm saying Bucky will win. Play him for keepers, Bucky. You can get that blue mib away from him."

"We don't play for keeps," Willis objected. "We only play for fair."

But the circle of watchers had decided they wanted the excitement of a game played for "keeps," instead of for "fair," in which case marbles are returned to their owners.

Bucky joined them. "Come on, Willis. For keeps this time."

Willis closed his eyes against the sight of the ring of bright marbles. Closing his eyes was a mistake. It pulled him back into the present where he was dizzy and hurt and weak. He opened his eyes and focused once more on the marble shoot.

They had been eleven that spring, he and Bucky and Jimmy Johnson, a year marked in memory because Bucky and his family had moved away that summer.

He could see all the marbles, clear against sky and tree branches above him. Playing for keeps! If he had known, he wouldn't have put out that sky-blue mib. There were two others out there that he didn't want to lose; one was a special shade of green like the first leaf of summer and one was mixed red and gold. They were out there now. He couldn't take them back. And he'd just sound like a coward if he insisted on playing for fair when Bucky and everybody else wanted the game played for keeps. Willis thought that for him it would be enough to win. He wasn't interested in taking Bucky's hoodles and mibs, but he didn't argue. He just eyed the lag line and gave it his best shot. Then Bucky shot.

"Bucky's closer," someone in the little crowd of onlookers called.

But Bucky said, "Measure it."

Willis was closer and had the right to go first. How was he supposed to have a chance to win when everybody was rooting for Bucky?

Willis took his shooting position, carefully chose his spot, and then knuckled down. One knuckle had to touch ground right up to the moment the shooter left the hand.

"No h'isting!" Jimmy Johnson warned.

Willis ignored him; he knew enough to keep his hand down.

"No hunchin'!" Bucky laughed to show his advice was a joke.

Willis's eyes moved over the ring, estimating distance, choosing a target, aiming. Knuckle down, hand steady so it couldn't hunch forward, he shot. Bucky's black agate marble, his "aggie," was propelled from the ring. Willis reclaimed his shooter, took aim again and this time bagged his own green marble. In rapid succession he took two more of Bucky's marbles. He now had four marbles. To win he needed three more. He took aim, but the shooter slipped from his fingers before he was ready.

"Slip!" he called and reached to retrieve the shooter for a second try.

"No slip!"

"That was no slip!" the watchers called.

"If it doesn't go more than ten inches, it's a slip," Bucky intervened. "Let's measure it."

"I'll measure it," Jimmy said and pounced on the shooter sending it flying out the other side of the circle. "Anyway, it *was* more'n ten inches."

"Yeah, ten inches at least," somebody else said.

Willis didn't mind giving up his turn when he lost it fair, but he didn't like being cheated out of it. Now there was no way to prove a slip. He picked up his shooter and moved back to let Bucky have a turn.

One—two—three, Bucky shot straight and picked up three marbles in a row, two of his own and one of Willis's. He took aim at Willis's mib with the snow swirls in it. It spun clear of the ring. He took aim at the red and gold marble Willis thought of as "fireball." The shooter hit it hard and took it out of the ring. Two more and the game would be Bucky's.

"Atta boy, Bucky."

"Knuckle down."

Bucky aimed and made a square hit on the sixth marble in a row.

Willis thought Bucky was a sure winner. A cloud over the sun cast the ring of marbles into darkness. For a moment Willis knew again that in reality he was lying on the forest floor with his life's blood slowly draining away. Time was passing. Help wasn't coming.

The shadow shifted and the ring of marbles reappeared. Willis saw that Mary Ellen had pushed through to the front of the circle of watchers. Hers was the shadow that had fallen over the ring.

Bucky looked up at her too, but Mary Ellen kept her eyes on the three marbles still lying inside the circle. She looked very solemn.

Bucky knuckled down, took aim, and fired his shooter into the ring. It missed. Without a word, he picked up the shooter and moved out of the way.

Willis shut out everything else. He could still win if he'd just concentrate. He settled his shooter just right on the curl of his index finger, hit it with his thumb and saw it take out a marble. He now had five marbles.

He fired again and collected his sixth marble. A stir went through the spectators. Willis and Bucky now each had six marbles. Only Willis's blue mib was left in the ring. If Willis missed this shot, Bucky would win for sure. Willis didn't care so much about winning any more. But he cared about that sky-blue mib. And he cared about Mary Ellen. Of course, Bucky did too. Her showing up like that was probably why Bucky missed his seventh shot. No, Willis didn't care so much about winning, but he hated to lose in front of Mary Ellen.

Now there was just one marble left. If it wasn't Willis's on this shot, it would be Bucky's.

A jostling for position ran through the spectators.

"No hunchin'!"

"Don't h'ist it now!"

Willis lifted his head and for a wonder Mary Ellen met his eyes. For a long moment, he saw her eyes as blue as the sky-blue mib he stood to lose.

Somebody said, "Knuckle down, Willis."

But Mary Ellen didn't say anything.

"Get it, Willis!"

Somebody was rooting for him after all. Mary Ellen's solemn face eased into a smile, and Willis knew that the voice in the crowd wasn't the only one on his side.

And Bucky saw the smile too. He moved forward, clapped Willis on the shoulder, and said, "Take your best shot, Willis!"

And Willis did.

The shooter seemed to move in slow motion. It made

solid contact with the last marble and the marble sailed toward the edge of the ring.

For him to win, it had to go out and the shooter must leave the ring too. If the shooter stayed inside the ring on this last shot, that final marble would be put back and Bucky would get another turn.

The marble rolled over the ring and away. And the shooter followed it. Willis had won.

"Good shot!" Bucky said and sounded as if he meant it.

Willis carried his marbles in a leather drawstring bag. He took them out and counted them several dozen times that spring, over and over, admiring their colors and the way they caught the light. He played and lost and played and won. But in each game he put aside the marbles he had won from Bucky so he couldn't lose them to someone else who might want to play for keeps.

When Bucky came to say he and his family were moving away, Willis knew he'd lost his best friend. The night before the Webbers were supposed to leave, Willis wrote a note that said, "I didn't want to play for keeps." He tied it to his leather bag of marbles, with all the marbles inside, and left it by Bucky's front door.

The first thing next morning he went back again to say goodbye. He was too late. Everybody was gone and Willis had never been sure Bucky had gotten the marbles.

He wished he could see old Bucky now. He'd like to tell him that when you're dying you don't always relive your whole life, that the one thing he'd relived was that marble game. Bucky would know which one.

*   *   *

Through light and gloom, horses approached, and someone shouted, "There's ten or a dozen Rebs here. Check 'em for survivors!"

Willis opened eyelids that were heavier now. The ring of marbles, bright as the sun, was blotted out once more. Only this time it wasn't Mary Ellen's face between him and the light. It was somebody in blue who was holding his bayonet poised above Willis.

To the sun-haloed face, Willis said, "It's your turn, Bucky. Take your best shot."

A dumbfounded Union corporal deflected the force of his blow and sent his bayonet into the ground.

"We'll take this one in," he said to the man beside him.

"Begging your pardon, Corporal, but the colonel said no more wounded prisoners. We ain't got the beds for 'em."

"We've got a bed for this one. He's an old friend." Then speaking just to himself, Corporal Webber added, "Though how he knew me behind this beard and him delirious, I sure don't know."

Later, when Corporal William Webber stooped beside a camp bed in a tent full of sick and wounded prisoners, Willis asked, "Why'd you spare me? This is supposed to be a war, y'know."

"Yeah, I reckon it is," Bucky said, "but it wasn't my idea to play for keeps."